www.trafford.com

North America & international
toll-free: 1 888 232 4444 (USA & Canada)
fax: 812 355 4082

Deliberance

Love Across
the Beaten Path

LORI ZAPANTA

Contents

To My Friends And Family

To my beautiful daughter Sonte Alena. The profound love I have for you continues to grow each and every day. You have been a true blessing to my life.

To my significant other and the father of my child, Max Newton. You have given me the greatest gift anyone can ever give.

To my mom, Kathy Harvey and to my Step Dad Rick Harvey for always being there for me no matter what is thrown our way.

To my grandfather, Roger Bedigrew, for being the best role model I could ever have. You have exhibited not only what a hard worker looks like but what a hard worker can accomplish and its benefits. I have always aspired to be like you.

To my niece, Kimberly Hoffman, you will always be close to me regardless of time or what happens in life. Gordy will always love you with all of her heart.

To Sonte's God Parents, Joanne and Richard Larsen. Our family is so grateful to have you in our lives.

To my wonderful friend Wilmarie Ortas, you have been a blessing to my life.

To my friend Sue White, I am so grateful we met and hope we stay in contact for many years to come.

ACKNOWLEDGEMENTS

I wish I had enough space to acknowledge everyone but that could be an entirely separate book.

I would like to thank Matthew Whitley of 3littlepigsproductions.com for giving me the idea for the title of this book. You are a great friend and you gave me the courage to keep writing this book even when I became skeptical of my talent.

Ashley Theuring (formely Ciraulo Stuart), I am so glad we met many years ago and all the time I have spent with you has been very precious to me. You are a great friend and a great person. And, your husband who I like to refer to as Sammie is wonderful too.

Deborah Hill, for reading my book prior to editing and allowing me to spend time with her beautiful daughter Ryeese.

Tami Muma, you have been a great friend to me for the last 15 years. You are always there to support me. I love you.

Thanks to Michele Jong for giving me feedback on my book prior to editing and for being a great friend.

CHAPTER 1

Off to the South

It was the middle of November in California when a co-worker and good friend of mine asked me what I was doing for New Year's Eve. I did not have anything planned because I just got out of a relationship that was ending in a divorce. My friend was going to see her long distance boyfriend in The South for an entire week. She and I had the week between Christmas and New Year's off so I thought what the heck. I could use a break from the full time enrollment I had at Pity University and watching excessive reruns of divorce court hoping to learn something for the upcoming doom resulting from the "d" word.

She called me from her desk at work, even though we sat right across from each other to whisper;

"Want to go with me to The South for New Year's, it will be fun?"

"I don't really have anything else to do, so why not." I said.

"Book your tickets with me soon so we can get the same flights and sit next to each other on the plane." She said.

"Are you sure you don't mind me being a third wheel with you two?" I said.

"Of course not, Mick and you talk on the phone all the time and we all will get a long great." She said.

We planned our trip with excitement, her more than I. I just wanted to get away from my normal boring routine of going home after work eating dinner by myself, hanging out with my cats, watching the occasional television show and going to bed alone.

It was quite the surprise to my good friends that I could leave my exciting life behind for an entire week to hang out with a happy couple somewhere in the rural South. The one requirement that I had was that no one fix me up with anyone while I was on vacation. I specifically told Dana to advise her boyfriend Mick not to set me up with any of what he thought would be eligible bachelors.

I called Dana the night before the trip so I could find out what she was packing and hoped that she remembered something I had possibly missed. She was giddy with excitement knowing that she was finally able to see her boyfriend again.

"I feel like I am forgetting something." I said.

"If you forgot anything we can always get it there if you need." She said.

"I can't wait to get out there—we are going to have so much fun." She said

"I am going to call Mick to see if there is anything else we should bring. I will call you back if I have anything new to tell you." She said.

She got to call Mick and I was left to consult with my two cats. The one thing I was afraid of was the fact that the weather was known to be unpredictable so I had to pack enough for layering just in case.

The flight out there was quicker than I thought. Dana and I were sitting next to each other talking about what we were going to do and she told me about her prior experiences with Mick and how much fun they had. Surprisingly enough there were no crying babies and no children kicking the backs of our seats. All and all the flight was a success.

The plane landed and Dana was so excited that she practically pushed people out her way just to get to baggage claim to see Mick. Mick was waiting for us with flowers—for Dana of course. I smiled and enjoyed her happiness as I remembered how my ex would buy me flowers once upon a time.

I couldn't help but think about the cost to all of this happiness. The cost of her smile at the airport resulting from his flowers only to end in distance and downtimes they had to endure when they were apart in their home states. It seemed unfair that they had to spend hundreds of dollars every few months and several hours on a plane just to get limited quality time. This thought made me really appreciate those I knew who were close in proximity to me. I no longer felt that it was much of a burden to drive thirty-forty five minutes to see someone knowing what they went through.

We drove to the small town where Mick lived and got settled into his apartment. The car ride seemed to take as long as the flight. Our view pretty much consisted of empty field after empty field with the occasional horse or barn. I was expecting to see Ma and Pa Kettle standing in a field watching us go by in amazement that a car was actually present on the empty road.

I sat in the back seat and tried to relax my head on the side of the seat only to be bumped to death by one of the tires. The right back tire appeared to be off of alignment and the bumping was accompanied by a mild constant thump. No flowers for me and now I pick the wrong side of the car.

By the time we arrived at his house we were in desperate need of cleaning up. Our hair and make-up took a toll while trying to lean up against the seat on the airplane attempting to get some rest before our weeklong trip.

After cleaning up a bit and taking a brief tour of his apartment, Mick took us to a restaurant that I had never heard of. It contained a massive salad bar with an abundance of side options and a variety of meat options such as beef tacos and enchiladas. Usually those types of places where we were from only included organic items most of which were vegetables. The meat dishes at this place provided an inviting allure.

Dana and I were so hungry that we just dove right into the salad bar and went to town. We both loaded our plates in a way that an onlooker would think that we had no idea it was all you can eat. I think our overwhelming hunger prompted us to grab as much as we could in the event that someone else would come by and rob the salad bar of its amazing pickings.

Mick provided some details about the small town we were in while my mind wandered about what I was going to get during my second round at the salad bar. It is sad to realize how exciting the salad bar was to me knowing that it was probably the most satisfaction I would have on this trip apart from Dana's wonderful company. She bonded with Mick as I bonded with the infamous salad bar.

Time flew by over the next few days about as fast as my short-lived college graduation ceremony. Once your name is called to cross the stage to get your diploma you realize that the several years of sacrifice came down to a quick 3 minute—at best—walk of fame.

One day in the middle of the week I found out that Mick attempted to fix me up with one his friends without my consent of course. I couldn't decide if he was doing more of disservice to me or to his friend considering I was just coming out of a bad marriage.

My marriage left me with a really bad taste for all men. I didn't care at that point if I intimidated a man, came off too strong, or even if they cared about my baggage from the past. I am sure I seemed like such a wonderful catch. I wondered how I could get out of this upcoming awkward situation. Would they find me if I sought refuge at my new favorite restaurant the glorious salad bar?

We ended up at a bowling alley where several young boys were chewing tobacco. I couldn't believe my eyes when I saw them chewing and spitting right in front of the adults. I wasn't sure if these adults were their parents or if they were just glorified baby sitters with no sense of responsibility.

This scene was not at all what I was used to and I was starting to wonder about the caliber of man that Mick would have us meet at this type of establishment. Dana, Mick, and I claimed our lane at the chewing tobacco salon and waited for the mysterious guest to arrive.

Part of me was hoping he would be cute and woo me so I could forget about my impending divorce and the other part of me hoped he would be so ridiculously ugly that I would just laugh inside at the very thought that this could be someone my friends would actually set me up with.

One guy with a mullet and a huge wad of chew in his mouth came walking towards our lane while my heart practically pounded itself out of my chest in mere desperation of finding an escape route. All I kept thinking was that I don't have a dip cup or whatever those things are called for men to spit into and I certainly didn't want to be with a man who needed one. My palms were sweating and thoughts of my ex seeming not so bad at this point shot though my mind at warp speed like a shooting star in the sky. I prayed like I never prayed before that this indeed would not be the guy. I mean, there were probably some really nice women on the other side of this bowling alley just waiting for their mullet prince charming to walk around the corner with his Dr. Skoal in his back pocket. I wiped the sweat from my hands in the event that I would actually have to shake his hand and that's when he walked right past us. Whew!

My pre-cardiac arrest was starting to come back down to a low simmer and then another guy walked our way. He was a nice looking man with no mullet and no chew. I was up at least two points with this guy. He ended up being the guy and a really nice guy at that. He was a little bit quiet but very polite and he seemed to have a good time.

Unfortunately I didn't feel the chemistry with him so our relationship would evolve into friendship at best. I would need someone who was more social than this. We had fun but really didn't talk much. Over a lifetime that would just drive me crazy. I would probably end up talking to myself or the cats resulting in being labeled the crazy cat lady.

Later that evening I found out that he too was going through a really bad divorce and that is why "good ol'" Mick thought we would get along. Yeah, let's stick the poor suckers with baggage together so they can contaminate each other's lives and not infect the wholesome ones. I tried not to take it to heart that I was now a statistic helping raise the percentage of divorced individuals and that my friends would see me soon as someone I hoped to never be—divorced. This vacation has got to get better.

CHAPTER 2

Getting to know you

Later in the trip I found out that one of Mick's friends called to say he was in town visiting his parents for the holiday when Mick asked him to join us the next day for New Year's Eve. What? I couldn't believe what I was hearing, great another guy for me to meet. I wasn't sure if my body could handle another cardiac arrest so I asked if this was a setup and Mick said no.

"This guy was not someone I would fix a friend up with because he is very busy and most people can only tolerate him for a short period of time." He said.

"Good, then I won't look too much into it." I said.

He kind of chuckled after saying that so I was not sure if he was trying to be funny or this guy was indeed the wrong type of guy for anyone. I took it as a hint and didn't care to ask any more details because the party was about New Year's and I wanted to kiss men goodbye if only for that one day and night. I also found out that Mick had yet another friend, friend #2 waiting in the wings to meet us at this party for round two of the bachelorette. Right about now I am thinking that Mick needs to focus on Dana and not on some poor schmuck like me who is in need of a guy break.

Mid-day Dana and I had arrived back from the spa where we had a nice relaxing bath in our separate spa suites, drank mimosas, and got a massage. This was all after we spent an hour at the gym where we pretty much completely wrecked any hairstyle that we started with that day. We looked pretty rough—relaxed but rough none the less.

When we got back to Mick's place Dana called dibs on the shower and took off as if her clothes were on fire. I had no chance of making it to the bathroom before her. She was a thick set woman with a 5 foot 11 frame. And, me being a 5 foot 8 body weighing in at about 130 pounds had no chance at any type of tackle maneuver. I was glad that Mick had seen me many times in the morning by now so I doubt my appearance was too alarming or offensive for him.

Mick's friend Peter who had called earlier showed up at his house before I had a chance to clean myself up. I was making a famous dip of mine on the stove when he walked in. I saw him from a distance and man was he tall. He was somewhat cute with his sandy blonde hair and his pouty lips.

He seemed a little bit intrigued by me as I caught him glancing over my way a couple of times. The only good view I thought he had at this time was my hard earned abdominal muscles that I worked for every time I was in the gym. Overall, I was glad that he would see me as a wreck and hopefully that meant I would be safe for the night with no potential of any advancements from his, "very busy—too busy for relationships" friend.

Before we left for the party we all went to dinner. Our waitress showed us to our booth seat when I looked at Dana and I whispered, "Do not sit on the opposite side of me, I don't want to sit next to this guy." I really thought our bonding session on the plane would have scored me some friendship points and she would make the boys sit next to each other. My luck wasn't much better at that moment than at the bowling alley a few days before.

So, as uncomfortable as it was Peter and I sat next to each other. And yes, he did seem very distant and to himself as the verbal description provided by Mick so clearly matched. What happened to the intrigue that it seemed he had for me at Mick's apartment? I wasn't sure if he was trying to be detached from the whole dinner date or if he was scared straight. For some weird reason I was hoping to at least get some kind of glance since I was all cleaned up with my makeup and hair done. Maybe I didn't look much better made up and all of these years of personal confidence was a farce.

Dana and I talked and talked as the dinner came and went with some ease—emphasis on *some*. My least favorite part of the evening was when Dana pulled out her digital camera to take a picture of Peter and me. Why would anyone want to take a picture of two absolute strangers with no hope of a future? He wasn't even my date so I shot Dana a look of disapproval without having any impact on her because she took the picture anyway.

When seeing that picture later I discovered that I was the only one leaning in towards him making me appear somewhat eager and needy—which I absolutely was not. Who was this guy and was he an arrogant prick or just really shy and do I care?

We drove to the party and once we entered the house and got acquainted with everyone I started to drink like a fish out of water. At that point I figured bachelor #1 didn't work out, bachelor #2 never showed up and what seemed to be bachelor #3 was staying at a distance.

I wondered if I wore the wrong perfume that night or if I was emanating the same scent that a female praying mantis does right before she kills her mate. Did bachelor #3 know this smell? Could he see the distasteful thoughts of men racing through my mind while I tried to rid myself of all the memories of my ex?

I must need to drink more because I should not be thinking this much. Drinking, here I come.

Every time I walked past Peter and saw him by himself observing the party I handed him a drink and made him drink at least some of it in front of me. I kept telling him to loosen up and have some fun. I could not tell if the isolation was of his doing or if he just felt out of place.

After making my rounds with Peter and drinking most of the night I was cut off from making my own drinks because apparently I was slurring and swaying when I walked. Did my friends not know that I was really doing impressions and that was a strut not a stagger? The designated bartender would tell me that they were making me liquor and coke drinks but I ended up with only coke. I must have been pretty drunk because by that point I couldn't tell the difference.

So, I consumed a few extra calories that year—next year (the next day) I was more than capable of making a resolution to lose them. I think I consumed at least two liters of coke just by itself.

When it started to get dark the guys went out to the back yard and set up fireworks. After the fireworks were prepped and ready to go everyone at the party hovered around excitedly to watch. Dana and Mick were arm in arm of course and I was standing in the back wondering why I didn't have someone at this special time of year. Instead of reminiscing about my days at Pity University I walked up to Dana on her bare side and put my arm around her arm. I figured I came all the way out here to this small town with no one the least she could do was show me a little love. And, I really did not want any of the single guys to get any ideas and try to prey on the limping drunk baby deer.

A few minutes later Peter walked up to me out of absolutely nowhere and put his arm around my waist. I melted! Before that night I could not even remember what it was like to be touched by a man that way and it felt damn good. Neither of us realized during that brief encounter that most of our actions were probably from the drunken stooper we both managed to master.

Peter and I somehow ended up attached at the hip the rest of the night wobbling together and laughing at almost everything even though most of it wasn't funny. Was this what an addict does with their pusher? Because, quite frankly, neither Peter nor I needed any additional alcohol and I was not going to be his "supplier" anymore.

Later in the evening we found ourselves out in the front of the house alone. He said he needed to get something from the car so I eagerly followed him outside. Again, this is the wild lion leading the wounded baby deer from the pack to gain the advantage. I had no clue. I stood sloppily on the sidewalk waiting for him to return from his car and thought to myself, why am I even out here with him aka the enemy. As drunk as I was I didn't care that it felt like only 30 degrees or the fact that I wasn't even wearing a jacket. I was hoping the cold weather would sober me up. He walked up to me after his infamous walk to the car to get "something he needed" wink wink and we talked for a brief couple of minutes. He then leaned in to give me a kiss—when all of a sudden the front door flew open and almost everyone inside started yelling, "Look they are making out in the front yard."

Well, the kiss never happened because of this major disruption. We both felt awkward after that and moved on with the evening. Sadly, after that incident we came to realize, we were not the only ones drunk and acting like a group of baboons in need of attention. On a positive note—no one was slinging poo so the night wasn't a complete loss—or, was it?

Peter and I stayed on the couch and tried to maintain a normal conversation for hours after everyone went to sleep. He rubbed my arm contently and stared at me as I told him stories about my life. I tried to hold my interest when he shared his stories as my buzz sunk in and I realized I drank a little too much before the wonderful non-alcoholic soda. I was hypnotized by his incredibly sexy southern accent.

We ended up saying goodnight as the sun started to rise and we both went to bed. I was sharing a room with Dana and Mick and Peter was blessed with a blow up bed in the middle of the front room. How was it that three people ended up in the same room while Peter got the front room all to himself?

I prayed as I entered the somewhat dark room that I would not get sick and be terribly hung over in the few hours to come and during our flight home. I went to lie down and Dana and Mick were already asleep consuming most of the bed. Dana was feeling cramped after I tried to secure a few small inches of what was left of bed space so she went and lay down on the floor and passed out. I ended up staying in the bed with Mick trying to lean as far as I could on my side in order to respect Dana's relationship and give me a clear path for the floor should the need to projectile vomit overwhelm me. This vacation was becoming quite interesting to say the least. Three male prospects and the only one I end up with in bed is my really good friend's boyfriend. Just my luck!

When I woke up the next morning I was happy to find that no weird stuff went on the few hours I was in bed. My fear, I would roll over and end up spooning Mick not knowing it was Mick. Luckily I stayed on my side and he stayed on his.

I felt so horrible that morning with only a few hours of sleep after consuming all of that liquor. I felt nauseas and exhausted. The friends who threw the party made us breakfast the next morning and I ate what I could. I figured I needed something to soak of all of that liquor. I really did not want to throw up on the airplane ride back. Talk about misery.

After breakfast Peter drove us back to Mick's apartment. He ended up staying at Mick's for a quick game of "whoop my ass in checkers." I was hung over pretty badly, hadn't played checkers in quite sometime and was quite smitten with him . . . who could concentrate under those conditions? I think I was still drunk because how could I still be interested in the enemy especially after my New Year's Resolution to disown all men. Peter was on his way out of Mick's apartment when he gave Dana and I a hug and told us to have a good trip back.

No request for my number and no request for an email. Are you kidding me? After all, I sort of sensed that he stayed longer at Mick's apartment just to spend time with me. Maybe that was my bruised ego seeking the attention it had lacked for so long. After he drove off I realized it was a good thing he didn't ask for any further information. He was after all in another state and I was in no way ready for a relationship of any kind in my current emotional status. Within a few hours we would be flying home and the day after that would be when reality would rear its ugly head again.

Mick dropped us off at the airport and said his goodbyes. Dana and I were so tired from staying up late the night before we were hoping to be able to sleep on the flight back. Even though I got less sleep than her I seemed to be more awake.

After the plane leveled off and everyone started to relax and fall asleep I saw something really weird out of the corner of my eye. Dana was at the window seat, I was in the middle, and a male stranger was sitting to my left on the aisle. It seemed like he was doing something with his finger and his face but I couldn't tell what. He was wearing a hooded sweatshirt and it was difficult to see his face. I was intrigued. I kept trying to look out of the corner of my eye in a sly way so he wouldn't catch me being nosey. That still didn't work. I couldn't tell what he was doing. I kept thinking maybe he had something in his eye or maybe he was picking his face because he felt some kind of bump, pimple, hair, etc. This went on for at least 10 minutes. I couldn't take it anymore.

I looked over in that direction as if I was looking for the stewardess and saw what he was doing. O my goodness, he was picking his nose. But that wasn't all.

He was picking his nose and then eating it. I thought to myself that I must be wrong. I must have seen something else. Maybe he was snacking on real food and I just caught him at an inopportune time where it looked as if he was participating in such a gross act. Could this really be happening? Do people pick their noses and really eat their findings? Is this guy going to touch the handrail in between our seats and leave remnants behind for me to accidently touch? I am thoroughly grossed out right now and can't move because the seat belt light is on. I must have looked over there 4 or 5 times and saw it over and over again. Why was I looking so many times? It's kind of like when you see something so outrageous that you cannot believe your eyes so you keep looking in the hopes that the view will change to what is considered the norm. Not in my case on this flight. I should have taken the window seat.

Dana has to see this. Not only is it gross but now I am starting to find humor in it because he has been in the act for over 25 minutes. Is he hungry? Is this an obsession for him? Maybe he gets nervous flying. The person on the aisle seat across from him is now looking at him too. I think he believes he is invisible with the hood on his head. He has done such a good job of trying to hide himself that he can't even see that people are looking at him in disbelief. I looked over at Dana to somehow motion her to check this out and she was knocked out asleep on the window. O' no, she cannot miss this. I bumped her arm with my elbow trying to wake her up. No luck. I bumped her again and still no luck. I tried to kick her under the seats and still no luck. Finally I saw the stewardess preparing the drink tray way at the front of the plane and used that as my excuse to wake her up. I moved over and nudged her while saying her name loudly. She jumped and woke up.

"The drink tray is coming, do you want anything?" I said as I gave her a look with my eyes rolling them to the left several times and trying to nudge my head in that direction.

"I don't know, I guess." She said in a quiet and confused tone after just waking up.

After a couple of seconds she caught on and looked over. Her eyes bulged in shock. She had the same look I had when this guy started on the picking marathon. I started laughing but tried to keep it to myself. The look on her face was well worth waking her up. The two of us tried to control our laughter and eventually tried to distract ourselves. It seemed like this guy was panning for gold. There was no stopping him. Every time I thought he would be done and give up the fight he was still in the race. I couldn't take it anymore. It was too bizarre for me to figure out and I just had to stop obsessing about this stranger.

Dana fell back asleep and I closed my eyes and tried to relax—anything at this point to divert my attention. I never did see the guys face under his hood. But, he did curtail the picking during the exit process when the plane landed. What a way to close out the memory of an out of town week spent with my friend. Mental note to self: next time take the window seat.

CHAPTER 3

Am I that easy to locate—
even out of state?

Monday came faster than my body and my mind would have liked. I walked into work and felt the comfort of being in a familiar place with familiar people. I had only thought about Peter a couple of times after leaving so luckily work wouldn't be interrupted by incessant thoughts of what could have been or what will be. Today was the first day of the rest of my life. I was starting over and giving it the optimism it deserved.

I checked my email at work and saw this unfamiliar name pop up. It was Peter emailing me at work. What? How? And, most importantly Why?

I paused for quite some time wondering if I should even open it. What good could come from a long distance friendship or relationship? Did I want to be exactly where my friend across the office was in her life—missing her boyfriend every day she couldn't see him. What about all of the money and time spent at airports just to see each other for a weekend? Was

I capable of having this type of relationship and did I even want to have this type of relationship? Did I really want to give thousands of dollars to the airline companies? I do not even have stock in any of these companies? Should I look into that first to see if the return is worth a possible investment—if that is what you can call it? Even if the friendship or relationship didn't work out then at least I could make a profit off of the money spent during the process?

I quickly went over to Dana's desk and told her about the email.

"Peter emailed me, what do you think?" I said.

I think I interrupted her daydreaming about Mick. She smiled at me in a very perplexing way.

"You should read the email and respond to him." She eventually said.

"Who knows . . . . you never know what will happen. If it is meant to be." She said.

This was by far her favorite phrase, "If it is meant to be." I used to wonder what that meant . . . if it's meant to be. How do you decide anything if it is meant to be? Doesn't that mean things will just automatically happen? How does anything automatically happen if you don't take some kind of action? Is this some kind of thinking from Buddhism or the Dali Lama? I thought she was a Christian? Our conversation was short because we were, after all, at work.

I made it back over to my desk and opened up the email. From what I could tell he seemed very intelligent and nice. I liked the fact that he appeared much friendlier in the email than in person. Maybe this was due to the fact that he wasn't sitting right in front of me and several other people and no one was around to judge him or us. I figured if nothing else maybe this could turn into a good friendship and it could be a nice distraction from my uneventful life.

His email read:

"Hello from the frozen north eastern tundra. How was your trip back? I hope you are doing well and I had a great time with you over the holiday. Take care, Peter."

I emailed him back and said, "How did you get my email address? This was very crafty of you. It was nice spending time with you too. I hope you made it back home ok."

I left it short and sweet because I had no idea where this would go and I was not going to encourage him in anyway. Per Dana, if it is meant to be.

After responding to his initial email our emails eventually turned into correspondence a few times a week, which then eventually turned into phone calls. It was so nice to talk about the different states we were in and the different things to do. The discussions flowed very easily and I didn't have to get him drunk in order to open him up. He seemed so interesting and knowledgeable. I started to look forward to the almost daily correspondence. I could tell that he missed talking to me when we went more than a day without talking. If we went more than one day he was much more enthusiastic when we spoke. He would always tell me we needed to catch up—even if it was only a couple of days.

My mind and heart were at a conflict because my heart wanted to see where this would take me and yet my mind was thinking how could anything good come from a relationship with such distance involved.

One night we were talking on the phone and somehow we started rating our appearances in the numerical sense. This was not such a good idea I later found out. I had men in the past tell me that I was a perfect 10. They could have easily said that to me because they were trying to be nice even if I was close but not quite a 10. They could have given me this top rated title because they actually believed that I was of the label 10 caliber. Regardless, I may not be a perfect 10 but I think I am at least above the midpoint in the range of 1 to 10. So, Peter was asked the infamous rating question and he answered. I even tried to make it a little bit easier on him by giving him a larger range of 1 to 20.

"So, what number would you rate me between 1-20 for appearance sake?" I asked.

"Fourteen" he said.

The answer was not so good. He rated me much lower than I expected which made me think that he may not have been that attracted to me after all.

"What made you say a 14" I asked.

"I am just being honest." He said.

He kept going on about why he chose that number and at one point it got really good—about as good as a semi-truck running over one of your legs.

"I have seen many beautiful women and even though you may not be as good-looking as them you probably have other qualities that make you attractive." He said as if this would make me feel like a prize.

I couldn't think of any abnormalities that would provoke such an answer. I didn't have a uni-brow, mustache, or a random long thick hair protruding from my chin. Aren't those dead ringers for guys to run the opposite direction? I didn't have a wandering eye or even a hair lip. Not that any of these would be a deal breaker necessarily and not that anyone having any of these qualities aren't great people—I just couldn't think of anything that would assist in the rating of 14 out of 20. Isn't this rating a 70% and isn't that a C grade? Not sure that I am proud to be a C.

In fact, I have one quality that most of my friends and strangers notice—my eyes. My eyes are a very pale grey and a lot of strangers say they look like husky dog eyes. Not sure if that is a compliment but I like those dogs and I like their eyes so I will take it as a compliment. Even Peter said that he thought my eyes were very unique when we met. Didn't that score me some additional points? Not quite sure why I am even so disappointed by the 14 rating but it sure did get under my rosacea infested skin. Ok, I don't have rosacea either but I will make something up just to ease my pain.

During the rest of the call I had to distract myself from the burning feeling of inadequateness in the attractive category and the nonstop feeling of wanting to go for his jugular. Since I knew that he hadn't been in too many relationships I let this one go (after giving him a bad time of course) and moved on to the next subject. Thanks to this fun exercise we sure weren't going to have any rating questions on the horizon for either one of us. Women always say they want their man to be honest but not so much on this one. I have to refer back to what my mother used to tell me, "be careful what you ask for?" I really should have been more careful.

We continued to talk and email each other and in fact a couple of months into the friendship we were corresponding sometimes more than a few times a day. We started asking more specific questions about each other's life and history. We were trying to determine if there were any red flags or issues. Red flag number one for me was the blatant honesty in the rating system exercise. Does he know the difference between being too honest and just plain out offensive? Can he learn the difference with time? Can old dogs really learn new tricks?

We seemed pretty compatible in this phase of the relationship—phase "developing friendship." I even found out that he had a lot of what I like to call "OCD" (obsessive control disorder) moments. He had a particular way of cleaning and preparing his dress shirts for work. He didn't like the way the drycleaner would starch and iron them so he did that part himself. I should have asked what he rated the drycleaner—maybe then I could have had company in the "low end of the scale" club. Back to the shirts—he would usually starch his shirts on the kitchen table until they were fairly wet and then lay them flat in a plastic bag overnight—sealed of course. Then, the day after starching he would take them out one by one and iron them.

Sometimes I would talk to him while he was ironing and it seemed like it would take him hours. I wasn't sure if this was because we were on the phone and it was difficult for him to multitask or if he just had that many shirts. After he ironed each one he would hang them up very carefully on a hanger with each arm folded over the other. When the entire process was complete he would walk them very gently back to their home (i.e. the closet). I thought the worst that could come out of this obsession would be that he could iron my shirts and I would save money normally spent at the drycleaners. What would I do with all of that money?

His discovery for me was that I was very particular about people keeping their word. I had told him that my ex made several promises over quite some time that he rarely kept. I advised him that I would trust him of course until he gave me reason not to. Also explaining that it was just better at this point not commit to even the smallest thing if he was unsure. I wanted to avoid any premature misunderstandings or rash judgments. He agreed to respect my wishes and went on to assure me that he was usually pretty reliable. When I heard him say those words I wondered if he was being more confident in himself than honest. Only time will tell. Regardless, I made a promise to myself that I would at least give him the chance—after all he was not my ex so why should he have to suffer for someone else's mistake.

CHAPTER 4

Spring Break . . .
is this a rash decision?

S̲o, we decided to take the next step in our relationship. We started talking about seeing each other and who would visit whom. This thing was really happening—we were starting an actual long distance relationship. I wasn't too sure if I could even believe that I actually allowed myself to fall victim to something I swore I would never do because of the possible risks and disappointment. And, have I bought any stock in the airlines yet?

When we were finalizing our plans he began to act a little apprehensive about the trip. Here we go I thought . . . now that we are actually putting the plan to work he is going to get cold feet and back out before I have the chance to. Boy, would I hate to be dumped by someone I only met once and by someone who seemed to want this more than me.

Due to my inquisitive nature I started to ask him if there was a problem and if he wanted to delay the upcoming trip or even postpone talking about it.

"No" he said "I am really looking forward to seeing you."

So, then I asked the next obvious question,

"Why do you seem reluctant?" I said in a neutral tone.

"Because there was something I was going to tell you but didn't know if or when I would be ready to share it with you." He said.

Of course my mind was racing with every possibility from "I have herpes" to "I don't think we should have sex during our trip." The possibilities were endless as to what secret he could be keeping. I tried to reassure him that I would not get angry with him nor judge him (providing of course it wasn't herpes) but he wouldn't budge.

So, then I tried the guilt trip option and said, "If it is something I should know before inviting you to my home and possibly getting intimate then I think you should tell me."

Eventually he gave in and told me something I didn't even consider.

He said, "I'm a virgin—are you happy now?"

I thought to myself—how could a thirty-year-old man who is pretty attractive and very intelligent be a virgin. O' man was this going to be a fun conversation and a fun trip if we do decide to proceed with the relationship.

"I come from a very strict Catholic family and I have always either been in school or worked very long hours." He said in a somewhat embarrassed someone aggravated tone.

"My busy lifestyle did not allow me to spend enough time with someone in order to know them well enough to get intimate." He said.

Wow, is all I kept thinking as he tried to convince me he wasn't gay or an undeserving geek. Not that either is a bad thing but if he is gay he is coming to see the wrong person. I just wanted to know what was going on. Would we have enough time to get to know each other intimately during our trip to make the sex worthy if we do indeed have sex? Do I take control and lead the way so he can follow? Would he want to lead because he is the man and would he be leading us in the right direction without any prior experience? What was I getting myself into at this point? Do I really want to do this? Isn't this the highest form of flattery when a guy is going to possibly surrender his virginity? Why won't my brain stop with all of these incessant questions?

"I do not care that you are a virgin and we will figure things out if/when you come out to visit." I said trying to reassure him.

He was still somewhat upset that I persuaded him to tell me his secret because I guess he wanted to just spring it on me when we actually met again. After getting past the initial shock of the virgin status we moved on to other topics. Then, shortly after the cat was out of the bag we started opening up to each other more about sex.

"I watch a great deal of porn so I can familiarize myself with the act when I do decide to do it." He said while laughing.

"Really, well that's good I guess." I said.

"My friend Jessabel is calling me on the other line can I call you back later?" He said

"Sure, no problem." I said.

I wondered if there wasn't a book out there or a video of some sort that this guy hadn't read or referenced in order to self educate. Would this type of exercise constitute as independent study? If he was being honest about the porn than I guess it was better than him watching the nature channel. I couldn't imagine how his first time would be if he was trying to mimic a mating ritual of some odd animal of sorts. Doesn't the black widow kill her mate after the act? I don't want to be part of that.

When we started getting comfortable talking about sex the next sex topic came into play—phone sex. I thought maybe it would be a good idea for us to express ourselves in this manner as an introduction if you will before the actual visit. He also seemed very interested in the idea. We started with the stories and went all out. Some nights we would be on the phone for hours—one hour talking and one-two hours having wonderful phone sex.

It wasn't quite like the real thing but heck it had been at least a year and a half since I had any action involving another person and he apparently had never had this type of interaction. To say the least, it was awesome! I would wake up so tired the next day for work but I didn't care because there was a smile on my face and I felt so liberated. Sometimes I would find myself in a daze at work remembering the stories and how close we seemed even though the distance was so significant.

It was a good thing Dana and I worked in cubicles outside of the direct view of our boss. She would sit and daydream about Mick and I would daydream about Peter. We were two lost souls trying to figure out where we were headed and how to make our situations more permanent.

Since Peter and I were having such intimate moments on the phone we decided to make plans for a trip. The trip was scheduled during spring break. We actually devoted an entire week toward "getting to know you" in my hometown. The relationship was evolving and we both seemed to be ok with it. He bought the plane ticket and I requested the time off from work.

Over the next few weeks before the visit I noticed the tension building and the anxiety growing. I must have cleaned my apartment twenty plus times right before his arrival and washed my car from top to bottom. Little did I know that I was actually pretty good at washing cars. Not quite like his OCD with his shirts but pretty close.

The day came when he was on his way. I went to pick him up at the airport around 11:00 pm and got there so early I had time to read a magazine I brought just in case. I certainly didn't want him to walk down the escalator and not know where to go or wonder if I had chickened out. I had to call Dana on my cell phone when I saw that a plane had landed and noticed people coming down the escalators. The airport was pretty much empty except for the last few flights coming in for the evening. Dana coached me through my anxiety-ridden state while I waited for him to come down the escalator.

"I am so nervous Dana, do you think it is too late to back out? I said somewhat freaking out.

"Of course is it too late for you to back out. You will do fine and you guys will have a lot of fun. Don't worry about it." She said.

"I see him, I see him, and he is wearing the same shirt he wore the day we met," I said to Dana as my heart nearly pounded its way out of my chest and took the next flight out of there.

"I am so excited for you guys." She said.

"Thank you for talking to me until he got here. I am going to go now. Talk to you later."

He found me in the crowd of people waiting for other passengers and smiled . . . I smiled back. When he got to the end of the escalator I started walking towards him praying that I wouldn't trip on the walk over to him. He came up to me smiling from ear to ear and gave me a huge hug. I hugged him so tight hoping my heart would remain on the inside of my chest cavity. I could feel him smelling my hair during the hug. I was extremely glad that I had time to wash my hair. As busy as I was with all of the cleaning I almost had to resort to hosing myself off when I became pressed for time.

When we finished hugging I gave him a rose that I bought for him earlier that day. Then, we made our way over to the baggage claim to retrieve his luggage.

I felt like a giddy schoolgirl standing next to this 6 foot 5 man—me being only about 5 foot 8. We were both so happy at that moment that I wished time would stand still and let us soak up every bit of it as long as possible. We kept smirking at each other at the baggage claim. We both were nervous but we didn't let that ruin the moments together before we left the airport.

"How was your flight?" I asked.

"Fine." He said.

We walked to the car with his luggage and not much was said. I tried to help him put his luggage in the trunk but he, as a gentleman, wouldn't let me help.

We both got into the car and smiled again at each other once again. I wasn't sure if he was waiting for me to do something or if he was just waiting until we got back to my place. I waited a couple of extra minutes to see if he would kiss me and nothing. I started the car and we were on our way to my apartment. I couldn't believe that he was here for an entire week. This was crazy.

We drove into my apartment complex and my stomach dropped—we are here, now what do I do? The walk to the front door was almost as nerve racking as the walk to the car at the airport. I showed him where he could put his things and took him on a tour of my huge 750 square foot apartment.

After the tour we sat down on the couch to talk and the awkwardness set in. He sat down right next to me— in fact so close that our legs were touching. Ok, now my heart is beating a mile a minute. Am I sweating? Do I have the word *nervous* written on my forehead? I think I was more nervous than he was and that was unusual considering that I knew he was the unseasoned one.

I wasn't sure what was going on. After all, he never did kiss me the night we met and that was New Years Eve—when everyone is supposed to kiss someone. New Years Eve would have been the perfect time to sneak it in and that would have been a good excuse. Now he is sitting so close that we are touching and in a place where we are the only ones present.

"So, your flight was good you say?" I asked again from the nervousness.

"Great." He said.

"Are you tired from spending all day traveling?" I said

"Somewhat." He said.

"The drive to the airport was good because there was little traffic." I said.

"That's good." He said.

I think we were trying to counteract the nervousness we both felt by making small talk. It was uncanny how we could talk on the phone for several hours at a time but then not know what to talk about once we were near each other.

It seemed like hours (really only about 10 minutes) before he leaned over to kiss me. We ended up kissing and making out for quite some time. He was such a great kisser. It seemed like we had so much chemistry and the built up tension sure did help improve the intensity of affection. We started to breathe a little heavy and we could tell that we were both getting weak.

Eventually I couldn't take it anymore and I said that I was going to bed. I wasn't sure that he was ready at almost midnight to lose his virginity and I wasn't sure that I was ready to break the year and a half record of celibacy—so, I left it at that and said goodnight. I went to bed and just laid there for quite a while. I couldn't stop thinking about the kissing and his sexy pouty lips. I couldn't believe that I felt so attracted and attractive to someone again. I forgot what the novelty of a new relationship felt like. Eventually my body gave out and I fcel aslccp.

The next morning came all too soon. We were in fact waking up in the same town after all of these months of separation. I wanted to call him in hopes that the call would reduce the amount of awkwardness that we were both experiencing. Maybe a phone call would enable me to calm my stomach enough to eat breakfast so I would have some energy and not pass out at some point in the day. He probably would think I was some freak calling him from my cell phone when he was only a matter of feet away. No need to start off the week with that label, as I am sure I have plenty of time to convince him some other way.

We needed to decide what we both would have for breakfast, lunch, and then dinner. I tried somewhat to pull myself together and look as decent as my bed head would allow before entering the kitchen and seeing him during breakfast. While I made breakfast I explained to him that I tried to eat as healthy as possible. I once had what I liked to call a "Nazi" personal trainer that ended up being a great friend of mine. She obsessively held me accountable for my eating regime during our many boot camp-like training sessions. She taught me that food is fuel not a luxury and if something did not have nutritional value then dump it like a really bad boyfriend.

From that point on in my life I became very conscience of what I ate—except for my famous Friday cheat days. Friday was the only day I allowed myself to eat whatever I wanted. And, to my surprise, because my body adapted to eating so nutritiously most other days I could not go over board or I would make myself sick. Needless to say, eating healthy was important to me so I thought it was an important discussion to have. Since he was from the South I wondered what kind of food he ate and if he would be disappointed that I didn't deep fry everything. No dirty rice in this house. My version of dirty rice was brown rice that dropped on the floor and exceeded the five second rule.

On came the old fashioned oatmeal with fruit, walnuts and non-fat milk in our coffee. I set the small bistro table I had in the front room, which forced us to be a lot closer than I would have liked that early in the morning. I felt as if I was only half a foot away from him and wondered if he could smell my wonderful morning breath. Do I have sleep in the corners of my eyes? Am I dropping below a 14 because I let him see me without any makeup on? He ate breakfast and didn't complain so I assumed it was acceptable for him—a couple of points earned on his side. Whew—we made it through breakfast, now onto the next major event of the day.

"What do you want to do today?" I asked.

"I am not sure, but I would like to go sightseeing at some point." He said while smiling at me.

"Ok, I can give you a list of things that we can see and we can map it out based on what you want to do." I said.

We couldn't decide what we wanted to do at that moment so we ended up lounging around on the couch and talking. We didn't talk about much and then we started kissing and all heck broke loose. You would have thought we were both going into cardiac arrest or having an asthma attack—the breathing was so loud that I was afraid my neighbor would think that something was critically wrong.

He grabbed my hand and took me down the hall into the bedroom. I couldn't believe how nervous I became. I thought we would at least want to see the town during the daylight before we started the courting session again. I had also hoped to get a shower before bumping uglies but I guess I should have just been happy that I got a shower so late the previous day. I mean, shouldn't the lifespan of a shower be dictated by the time in between them versus the actual day of the week?

I stopped the kissing and said that I needed to go to the bathroom. This was just a ploy to make sure I didn't have any unwanted odors anywhere and to sneak into his wardrobe for a nice surprise. I ran into the living room where he had his clothes and grabbed the shirt he was wearing the first time we met and when he came down the escalator at the airport a few hours prior. I put the shirt on and wore nothing else back to the bedroom where he was. When I came in he was sitting on the edge of the bed. I walked in with just the shirt and boy did his eyes open with surprise. He looked like a kid in a candy store and I was the candy. I walked up to him and he smiled as I started to kiss him.

"Are you ok with this?" I asked him.

"Yes I am." He said.

He gently moved his hand up my leg and to my "you know where." We were kissing very heavy now, he unbuttoned the shirt and dropped it to the floor, moved me over to the bed to lie down on my back and he got undressed. Holy cow I thought. Are we really going to do this? I was so nervous but also so excited to finally feel desired and pleasured. He moved over to me and looked at me like he had been waiting his entire life for this moment with me. I felt so special.

We were intimate for several hours and although I had the time of my life I noticed that he never climaxed. Did I wear the wrong shirt when entering the room or did I actually have some type of offensive odor lurking around that I missed in the bathroom?

"Is something wrong?" I asked.

"No, I am not quite sure why I can't climax." He said. "It's not that I don't want to—really!" he reassured me.

"Do you want to keep trying?" I asked.

"Yes." He said.

So, we continued to give it our all for a few more hours and still nothing. Finally we just gave up and decided to cuddle somewhere in between the make shift meals used for energy replenishment. He never did have his "moment."

The next day we were intimate again before we left the house and I was starting to wonder if this guy would actually get to see the sights before his departure. I wanted to be a good tour guide but I guess I was just giving him a tour of my body versus the town. We had now had many intimate moments and I was the only one walking away feeling as if I won a prize. I wasn't sure what to think while all of this was going on. It seemed like he was trying to enjoy himself but for some odd reason he just couldn't not have an orgasm.

Finally and I mean finally he climaxed during one of the two hour sessions later that week and man was I relieved. I was starting to wonder if I had lost the touch or if this guy had something against sex with me. I couldn't imagine what he was thinking. The pressure must have been horrible for him.

After the major accomplishments in the bedroom, the front room, and on the couch we finally saw daylight and made it out into the world. I took him to a few of my favorite restaurants, we ate dinner at my parents one night, and we went out with some friends another, then the rest of the trip was back indoors for more one-on-one.

My favorite night was when I was in the kitchen making dinner and he made a gorgeous fire and moved my bistro table near the fireplace so we could have a romantic fire-lit dinner. We ate dinner watching the fireplace and smiled at each other. We talked about our time together and how nice this week was so far. Later we cuddled on a blanket while drinking wine and talking about what else we might do. He brought my CD player out to the front room and played a nice country song while we slow danced for what seemed like an eternity. I felt so content at that moment I cried in his arms while he held me tight and assured me that everything would be ok. This guy was turning out to be quite the romantic. My heart melted. Could this week get any better?

Then, he got a call which he let go to voicemail. I asked him if he needed to take the call.

"No, it is Jessabel and I can call her later."

"Is she one of your good friends from home?" I asked.

"I met her after I moved to the Midwest through another friend of mine." He said.

"Does she have a boyfriend?" I asked.

"No." He said.

"You don't have to worry about her. She is more of a tomboy than anything. She doesn't wear makeup and she has a mustache. She is not very attractive." He said.

For now, I left it at that even though I was wondering who this person was, how long they had been friends, and if she had any ideas about my man. It was tough having a long distance relationship especially when you cannot make your presence known to all of the other women accessible to your man.

The end of the trip snuck up on us considering we didn't seem to do a whole lot outside of the house. He packed his things and I said goodbye to his button up shirt that I wore our "first night" together. I drove him to the airport and felt this overwhelming sadness as we walked into the airport. We stayed together as long as we could before he had to go through security. He sat with me on the airport bench until the very last minute holding my hand and smiling at me. And then I cried as I watched him ride up the escalator. I stood there until I couldn't see him anymore and then waited another few moments just in case he came back to give one more goodbye and then I left. The feelings I had that day were very foreign to me. It was a bitter sweet—I was happy but also so sad because I had to watch him leave knowing that we wouldn't see each other again for quite some time.

I waited until he was on the plane then I called him and left him a really nice message that he would be able to listen to once he was at his layover or when he arrived back at home.

"I hope you had a nice trip. I am glad you came out to see me and I will talk to you soon." The voicemail said.

He wasn't the only one who could be romantic. I am going to woo him like he wooed me while he was here. After all, he wasn't the only one to be desired in this relationship. I drove away from the airport crying yet trying to convince myself that this was not as bad as it seemed. Half way home I pulled myself together and forced my thoughts in the direction of the here and now—yet at the same time hoping he would call as soon as he got home.

We were back to our normal routine now that he was back in his neck of the woods and the distance between us became a sense of normalcy at this point. We were talking an upwards of two plus hours a day—it was a good thing we had unlimited minutes on our cell phones. We emailed each other when we could not talk, which was not often. Our constant conversations became a way of life for us. We would talk while we ran errands, while we ate, and when we got ready for bed.

I even got so used to his routine I could hear the floss container at night when he would prepare for bedtime.

He was in a time zone where he was three hours ahead of me so his routine was somewhat different than mine. I would go to the gym a few nights a week only to rush out so I could catch him before he fell asleep. I needed my daily dose of sweetie time you know. What was happing to me? I never thought in a million years I would be in this type of situation.

During one conversation I found out that Jessabel had asked him to go sailing with her and her family.

"Are any of her other friends going too?" I asked.

"No." He said.

"I think that sounds like she wants to spend time with you more than as friends." I said.

"No. It is just sailing." He said.

"Well, you do what you think is right but I am not convinced that she doesn't like you that way." I said.

"I don't think I am going to go anyway because I have things to do." He said.

Out of the blue Dana said that she had an interview in Mick's hometown. It seemed like she was getting pretty serious about her long distance guy. She had said many times that she would not move away from friends and family if she didn't have a ring on her finger—or at the very least a job. She emailed me at work;

"I really need you to come with me to Micks for moral support." She said.

She also wanted Mick and me to look for apartments in the area near her interview so she would have a place to live. She was adamant that she would not live with this man until they were engaged or married. This was one thing she would not budge on so she needed us to look for her potential new residence during her interview. Luckily, I worked in another department now so us calling in sick strategically on the same day would not set off any alarms with the "time off" police. The wheels were set in motion and we had our tickets. She was so crafty with the upcoming calling in sick routine that she started complaining at work about how she felt as if she was getting sick days before the trip and she also refrained from hanging out with anyone after work as well. Boy was she doing a much better job than I. I was just quiet for a few days. After all, she didn't give me enough advance notice to practice my sick routine to the fullest extent for it to be second nature.

Off to the airport we went. We popped our Dramamine and off we were into the blue skies. I sat in a seat where Dana would be the only one next to me. I had learned a little something from our last trip together. I asked her how she wanted to plan this trip.

"I would like you and Mick to look at apartments while I am interviewing." She said.

"Just tell me what you want in an apartment (washer and dryer, upstairs, downstairs, etc.). I said.

"No problem." She said.

We landed and arrived at the airport to find Mick with flowers—boy he really wanted her to move out there. I knew that Peter wanted to eventually end up there since this is where his family lived so I got creative by thinking that if she moved here we could be roommates. Then, Peter could come home to his family and me. How cute would that be for us to eventually be together in his hometown? All four of us would be so happy together and possibly in the long term even raise our children together. Man, this whole thing was panning out really nicely—I don't feel so bad about calling in sick on a Friday anymore.

The next morning Mick and I dropped Dana off at her interview and away we went to go apartment shopping. We saw some pretty amazing places. One place had what looked like a mini lake running through the entire complex with multiple bridges overlapping the water at various points. This body of water looking like a lake was actually the pool that branched off into many different directions. I had never seen any pool that large or with so many access points before.

Some apartments would allow you to use 5% of your rent towards the down payment on a house providing you used the same builder. I couldn't believe how positive this could be for Dana and me if we both played our cards right. Mick and I got tons of brochures and tried to remember which ones we liked and which apartments went with which brochures.

After all of the apartment shopping, Mick and I were getting into the car to go have something to eat before picking up Dana and my cell phone rang. It was Peter and he sounded really serious. For some reason he sounded totally different than any other time we had spoken. I felt my stomach tense up as I asked him what was wrong when he asked me a question that I had never been asked before,

"When was the last time you were checked for STD's?" He asked.

I gulped so loud I think my mother who was several states over could hear. I thought I was going to vomit even though I hadn't eaten much that day. Could this really be happening to me?

"Peter, I have been celibate for a year and a half and I think I would know if I had something." I said.

"You didn't answer my question, when was the last time you were tested?" He asked.

"It has been a while and I can't remember." I said. "Why are you asking?"

"I think you gave me herpes." He said.

Herpes—o' yes, herpes! I could not believe what I was hearing. I am in a different state trying to provide moral support for my good friend who is trying to get a job and an apartment and her boyfriend just got out of the car to give me a moment because tears are streaming down my face.

"Why do you think I gave you herpes?" I asked.

"I have painful bumps on the inside of my legs near my groin." He said.

I was so upset that this was happening I think the only thing that could have been worse is if I had to see the rash myself. I guess there are some benefits to long distance relationships after all. But, why then did I not have these symptoms? I continued to ask him questions and the conversation went from bad to worse . . . he eventually said,

"After researching this on the Internet, my mom and I think that it is herpes."

Immediately my mind went into a screeching halt and I said,

"WHAT?" "Your mom knows about this rash and about how we had sex—premarital sex at that?"

Ok, now I was going to barf—watch out glove box here comes whatever I ate for dinner last night.

"Why would you go to your mother before you came to me when it was me who you slept with not your mother?"

He tried to play the victim and say how scared he was and how he didn't know what else to do. I don't know, maybe go to the freaking doctors to see if they can examine said rash and provide an initial diagnosis before they run the actual tests. Maybe this would have given him some comfort knowing what the doctor thought it was. Then, maybe he wouldn't have had to send his mother and me into a frenzy. So, being the non-religious whore that corrupted this innocent 31-year-old man I asked the next best question,

"Have you even seen a doctor yet?"

"I can't get into a doctor's office until Monday because they aren't open on the weekend." He said.

So, let's call your mom and tell her that your slut of a girlfriend de-virginzed you and then gave you herpes.

Eventually the sadness turned to anger from the very thought that he would put his mother and me through this and jeopardize my friend's very important weekend just based on a rash without any facts.

"I need to think about what you just accused me of and I will have to talk to you later." I said.

I think I may have also said at one point, "You better hope those freaking tests come back positive for all of this trouble you caused." Ok, that wasn't the nicest comment to make at that time but gee whiz he couldn't have waited one-to-two days to drop the bomb on Hiroshima just to make sure there was real cause here? I mean a rash . . . I get razor burn all the time but do I dial 911?

So, I called my mom, it was after all call your mom day apparently. After explaining the entire story to my mom and actually questioning the fact that I may be an actual STD carrier/donor she said something that I hadn't thought of,

"Doesn't he know that he has jock itch, and why is he still a virgin?" She said.

"That's probably it. I guess I didn't think about that because I was in shock the entire phone call." I said.

"Don't worry about it. The tests will come back negative and then he will see how much he panicked for no reason." She said.

My mom was probably much calmer than his mom about the whole thing, my mom already knew I was a whore! No, really she knew that I had been married so she assumed that sex was involved at some point . . . or, maybe he divorced me because I wouldn't put out—ok, I have to stay focused here. She reminded me that Peter was an avid bike rider, he was on a basketball league, and it was pretty humid in his small town. She said that all of those conditions sure did make for a nice Petri dish/breeding ground for the infamous jock itch posing as herpes.

Somehow I managed to pull myself together and get through the rest of the weekend. I couldn't very well tell Mick about what had happened out of respect for Peter's privacy regarding his recent loss of virginity and his possible break out of herpes. I had to tell someone and Dana knew something was wrong. So, when Mick wasn't around I told her in the strictest of confidence.

"I cannot believe that." She said.

"Wow, he is a virgin. It is sad that he accused you of giving him an STD before having the facts." She said in a very compassionate tone.

I think Dana was almost as disgusted as I was. She made me feel so much better by understanding why my thoughts were so conflicted . . . I mean I did feel bad that he had a rash and that he was in pain, but if it was indeed jock itch then he put a lot of people through an extraordinary amount of stress for nothing. And, not to mention making me feel as if I had slept around so much that I was the donor of said disease. I wasn't sure if I could continue to see someone who conducted themselves this way in stressful situations.

Would I ever be able to meet his mother now? And, would I ever be able to forget how cheap and sluttish I am feeling at this moment. I really didn't have that many sex partners—REALLY! I was starting to wonder if this guy was mature enough to take this step in his life or if maybe he should have stayed a virgin until he got married. Then, if he pulled this on his wife she would have to forgive him or she would have a divorce on her hands—me, I was not obligated to do anything at this point in our relationship.

A few days after him seeing the doctor he got his test results. Was I scared? Absolutely not! Even the doctor had said that it looked minor when he was at his office visit but it was standard to check other alternatives just in case and run all possible tests. He called me with the test results and wouldn't you know it—my mom was right. It was jock itch. Now, who is the fool? I could feel the cheapness and sluttish feelings drift away but I was still severely disappointed as to how he handled the situation. Wait—Is that a pain in my ass? I am going straight to the emergency room!

CHAPTER 5

A trip to the Midwest

A significant amount of time had lapsed since the breakout discussion. Peter had eventually convinced me, after several long apologies that I should forgive him for his wrongdoing. So, being the bigger person I forgave him and let it go. We had another trip on the horizon planned and I was a little reluctant. I hoped that if we were intimate during this trip that he had some type of rash kit tucked away in case of an emergency and I was definitely going to delete his mother's number from the speed dial she apparently was on.

Before the trip to his place I had told him about this recipe I wanted to make for him for dinner. I raved about how delicious it was and also how healthy it was. We made a plan to go grocery shopping together and get the necessary items when I got there. We did our, what was now becoming a routine, normal packing phone conversation where we would help each other pack while I asked him what the weather predictions were and if I needed to pack anything specific. Who knows, he may have wanted to surprise me and take me to a nice dinner or dancing one of the nights we weren't cooking so I had to ask if I needed to bring a dress or something nice.

I was not too excited about traveling by myself. I was somewhat claustrophobic and every time I traveled previously I always traveled with someone. I even would fly my best friend with me over the years prior when I needed to travel somewhere for work (and pay her way since this was my inability to deal independently with my travels). My employer never knew she was there sharing the room they reserved for me. I always had a much better trip with her as a traveling companion and I was always ready for a seminar or more prepared for work meetings since I wasn't in a frenzied mode. She as well got to take time off from her four kids back at home.

I asked Dana to take me to an airport that was two and a half hours away and she gladly said yes. It was the only airport that offered a direct flight. I was pretty nervous—not only was I going to his home town for the first time but I was going by myself. What was I was thinking? Am I really sure I want to travel across almost the entire United States by myself and be picked up by a man I think I know well?

Dana dropped me off at the airport, hugged me and with a reassuring smile said, "Goodbye, you will be ok." There I was two and a half hours away from home with no ride back standing in an airport alone for the very first time. I stood at the curb watching Dana drive away looking like a puppy that just got abandoned.

I started to panic when I realized what I was doing and for whom. I called Peter and told him that I was starting to get nervous and he said,

"It will be ok, you are strong and the flight is a direct flight so when you land I will be there waiting for you."

"I am not sure I can do this?" I said about as scared as someone jumping out of an airplane only to realize that they left their parachute in the plane.

"This is the thing to do and it will be ok, I care about you and believe that the flight will go smoothly." He said in a reassuring tone.

I started to cry on the phone because I was so nervous. I asked God for a sign that this was indeed the right thing. As I walked over to the gate where I was supposed to depart from I saw a priest. I couldn't believe my eyes. I didn't think that I would have this obvious of a sign. Miraculously I started to feel better.

"Peter everything is ok and they are calling for us to board now." I said with a sigh of relief.

I lost sight of the priest until I boarded the flight when I noticed that he was sitting right in front of me. It couldn't get any better than this. At that very moment I thought, I can do this, I can really do this. And, I did make it through flight number 1 of many to come.

The trip out there went well even though it spanned over about an entire seven hour process. The more I traveled the more I realized direct flights were such a luxury—even if you were traveling for more than five hours. Every trip I sat at the edge of my seat when the first flight would land, race to get off the plane, race through the airport trying to find my connecting flight, then—if I had time, go to the restroom or get something to eat before the next flight took off.

By the time I landed in his town I had taken several Benadryl pills to combat the motion sickness and probably looked as if I was borderline road kill. I think he understood that an entire day worth of flying would make anyone look pretty beaten up and weathered.

After I got settled in his apartment we went to the grocery store. I was excited because I thought this was something couples do and we were after all slowing becoming a couple. I began to notice how frugal he was with his purchases and that made me wonder if it was budget related or this guy was just cheap. I gave him the benefit of the doubt by usually thinking he was saving up for something special or one day he would surprise me with a nice gift or a nice dinner—that still remained to be seen. We bought all of our items and headed out the door towards the car. He opened the door for me—another cute move and I thanked him with a kiss. I was so grateful I had decided to overlook the cheap judgment I made and got excited to start on dinner.

When we got back to his place he helped me unpack the groceries and I got started cleaning the vegetables and getting pans and a cutting board out. He hung out with me for a little bit while I was measuring and cleaning the food. I told him that he didn't have to do a thing for dinner because this was something nice I wanted to do for him. He was pretty intrigued by what I was making and asked a few questions here and there about the ingredients. At one point he even made a suggestion about putting additional spices in the recipe.

"I really wanted to make the recipe how I have made it in the past since it turned out so well. If we decide to make changes to the recipe we can next time based on how this one tastes for you." I said.

I thought he was listening to me as I continued to clean the vegetables over the sink, when I turned around there he was—adding his own ingredients to my dinner. Was this guy for real! I told him that I didn't want to add anything to the recipe because I was so anxious for him to try it the way I had made it prior since it turned out so well. Then, he started arguing with me.

"I really like minced onion in my recipes." He said.

"But the recipe doesn't call for that." I said.

"Yeah but wouldn't it be nice to try it this way?" He said.

"I thought I could make it the way the recipe called for first and see how you like it." I said.

"I was just trying to help." He said.

What? I thought to myself. This guy is arguing the fact that he should be able to deviate from the plan? I mean, I was making dinner for him and he didn't need to lift a finger. Most guys I know would be so grateful that their girlfriend is making them dinner that they would be figuring out a way to make it up to her after dinner rather than coming into the kitchen mid-way through the process and fiddling with her creation.

He was adamant about modifying the recipe to his satisfaction. So, eventually, when I realized that he was not going to stop and respect my wishes I left the kitchen.

"You can finish the dinner your way since you know how you want it." I said.

"Ok, I will stop." He said.

This comment was made as he was adding yet another ingredient to the recipe. So, I went into the living room, turned on the television, and relaxed. I was not going to get mad—even though I was a little bit upset that he wouldn't let me finish what I was doing. After being jet lagged and trying to do something nice for him with his constant interference I think I would have become really angry if I had stayed in the kitchen.

He came out to the living room and said,

"I am sorry, you should go back in there and finish and I will leave you alone."

This was after he already modified the entire recipe to his liking and after me repeatedly asking him to stop and let me finish. After I asked him several times to stop with no luck was when I casually walked out into the living room and decided that it was his dinner and that I was going to enjoy the dinner that he was making not the other way around. All I kept thinking about was the fact that I felt so ignored and unappreciated while in the kitchen.

I began to wonder if this was how he was raised, how his father is to his mother, or an unfortunate circumstance of being new to a relationship. Why does my mind race so quickly to a million thoughts? I guess I didn't want to feel that way again and my mind was trying to think of the culprit behind said action so we could deal with it and move on—hopefully with no reoccurrence.

"No, you can finish because I am done in there." I said in a calm voice.

I was too tired now to even care about how the food tasted or who made it. I just wanted to relax and get some home cooked food in me.

He got really upset that I would not go back into the kitchen. I guess he thought that I was so angry I couldn't even stand to cook him dinner—when in reality I was somewhat happy that I had a reprieve from slaving over a hot stove after my long journey. I also would not have to worry about him possibly not liking the recipe anymore—I mean, he did after all modify it to his liking so he is really the one to take any imperfections up with. Somehow the dinner was blown way out of proportion. He thought I was really angry with him and I knew he wasn't really happy with me. He, for some strange reason, thought that he should be able to do whatever he wanted in the kitchen regardless of my feelings; he should be able to apologize, and then decide that I would be the one to finish the dinner when he realized that he didn't want complete control after all.

I'm sorry, was I just a puppet in this scenario? Was I supposed to turn a blind eye to his adjustments or thank him profusely for improving the recipe beyond imagination? I come from the school of thought that when someone you care about asks you to do something—within reason of course—you respect their wishes—especially if they are doing something that benefits you. Maybe my school wasn't accredited and that's why that thought never got to him or his family.

We ended up eating dinner during the most uncomfortable silence I think we have had from the inception of our relationship. I could hear the crickets outside chirping excessively while we ate. Then, somehow we started trying to discuss the issue at hand. Was this really an issue? I thought when I was leaving him in the kitchen to finish the recipe his way he would be grateful and life would go on as if prior to the incident. But, for some reason he would not let go of the fact that I was upset by his actions and by the fact that I—what he called—threw a fit by sitting in the living room until dinner was done. The entire time I was in the living room I had a smile on my face and kept telling him that I was not angry and that I was sure dinner would come out fine even though he changed things up a bit.

The discussion turned into a fight and we eventually went to bed without even talking. This was the start of a really good trip. When lying in bed trying to go to sleep—my body so wanted to recoup, but my mind was racing a mile a minute—I couldn't stop thinking about what awaited us the next morning when we needed to make breakfast. Then, I wondered if there was anyway I could just fast the entire remainder of the weekend and not have to worry about the constant food supply my body had become accustomed to. Is there some kind of liquid diet that can carry me until my departure?

We managed to make up the next morning over breakfast. I think we just chalked the experience up to our nervousness and the fatigue factor. However, underneath the surface I think we were both wondering if we should consider the event substantial enough to warrant concern.

One day we met some of his friends for dinner. One of his really close friends was named Trevor. Trevor was an absolute dream. He was tall with dark brown hair, brown eyes, and was really fit. He was also shy which made him even more elusive. For some reason I just loved the time we spent with him. I thought he was funny and easy going. He also gave Peter a bad time for things that I too thought were just crazy. He once told me a story about how Peter was so determined to get the air out of a Ziploc bad containing left-over food that he took a straw saved just for this purpose to suck all of the air out before locking the seal. Most people do this with their hands but not Peter. I was glad to see that someone else thought that Peter had some oddities.

Most of the time I thought I was alone in the Twilight Zone.

The rest of the trip seemed somewhat normal. We went sightseeing and then went out to dinner a couple of times. I think he was dreading the check for dinner because he kept making comments like this place is expensive and we better get a lot of food for these prices. Not quite the romantic dinner I had in mind but at least the food was coming the way I wanted it and he wasn't allowed to go into the kitchen and fiddle with the food like he did before.

One person I did not meet on this trip was Jessabel. By the time the trip was nearly over it was too late to set something up. However, I did think it was somewhat odd of Peter to not bring her up or try to have us meet, especially if she was truly just a friend.

CHAPTER 6

To wine or not to wine

My birthday was fast approaching and Peter thought it would be nice to come out and see me for our next trip. I wanted him to meet and spend time with my best friend Taylor during my birthday celebration. Because I worked long hours and was busy most non-working hours I like to take it easy on my birthdays. My birthday tradition consisted of going to see a movie after a nice lunch and then going to my favorite Italian restaurant with Taylor. A year or two before this birthday my favorite Italian restaurant closed down so I had to find another destination spot for my birthday dinners. My other edible passion was sushi so I decided to make a local popular sushi restaurant the new birthday local. This sushi restaurant had a birthday wheel that you could spin to win various prizes ranging from a designer tea cup to a hefty gift certificate. By designer tea cup I mean a Japanese tea cup with the restaurant's name and logo on it. The logo was in cursive so it was pretty fancy.

Peter wanted to go wine tasting during this trip so we planned this event for the three of us. Taylor even surprised me the day of with a limo. It was a huge plus to have a designated driver during our wine tasting extravaganza. I certainly was not going to be a designated driver on my birthday weekend.

When we all arrived at a central location for the wineries we got a map showing each of the wineries and their locations for each area of the city. We mapped out the wineries we wanted to see and off we went. It was a very warm summer day with little to no breeze in sight. I think the weather topped out at about 90 degrees. We probably should have been hydrating ourselves with more than just wine but who was complaining. One of the wineries we stopped at had a beautiful huge wooden door that looked very old and antique like. There was a large creek in the front with a water fountain and green vines branching out all over the outside of the winery building. It was a gorgeous view.

When we got close to the water Peter attempted to throw me in as I wrapped my arms and legs around one of his tree trunk size legs. His legs were so tall he could drag my entire body wrapped around it like a monkey sitting on his foot. It was quite an amusing site.

We visited about five wineries that day all beautiful with their own personalities. Some had extravagant buildings with overwhelming entry doors while others had local artist pictures on display so you could enjoy the arts while wine tasting. Another winery had a huge picnic area outside their deli/restaurant where tons of visitors sprawled out on their picnic blankets to enjoy the sunshine. We saw fields of beautiful yellow flowers and rows and rows of grape vines everywhere. There was so much to see and one day didn't seem like enough time. When the day was over and the exhaustion from the heat set in we decided to end our limo experience. We wanted to finally get some much needed water and then dinner. Because it wasn't the actual day of my birthday I was flexible on the restaurant and left it up to Peter and Taylor. They decided on a casual restaurant closer to our home.

I thought the day was going well until we got to the restaurant. The dinner was good and I even went all out and ordered a chocolate milkshake. Then, all of a sudden some guy comes to our table and starts making balloon animals. We all thought it was pretty funny and even put in a couple of requests for a dog, flower, etc. We even jokingly asked him if he could make something really complicated like a famous building or a rocket ship and he said he would just stick to the dog and flower requests.

He tried to make small talk with us when flashbacks of the time I asked Peter to rate me on my appearance came flooding back into my mind. The balloon guy which we will name Jerk wad asked if Peter and I were together. We said yes of course.

"I would have never put the two of you together. He said.

"Why not?" We asked out of curiosity.

Remember, curiosity is what killed the cat and now I know why.

"You look much older than him. He looks like he is in his twenties and you are in your late thirties." He said totally oblivious that at that very moment I wanted to take his un-blown balloons, tie them together and wrap them around his scrawny little neck. I wasn't sure if he was trying to get us back from asking him to make something elaborate with his balloons that was way above his skill level. Either way this guy couldn't leave our table soon enough and there was no way he was getting any kind of tip from us—except for maybe a verbal tip advising him not to tell women they look old.

In my defense I had been drinking all day and the heat really took a toll on me. But, over ten years apart in age is what it seemed like he was suggesting? I was only two years older than Peter. This guy is a schmuck.

Then when I thought it couldn't get any worse trying to mask my pain from being labeled as a cradle robber or cougar Jerk wad decided to make me some balloon jewelry that looked like it came straight out of Bedrock. I was humiliated while Peter and Taylor tried to take my mind off of it. It didn't help that they laughed when I put the jewelry on trying to be a good sport, an old sport but a good sport. I am just going to chalk this experience up to the fact that Peter really does look young for his age. O boy, I can't wait for next year's birthday!

CHAPTER 7

Going to meet the parents

We started our normal phone routine again as the holidays approached. We started talking about what we were going to do for the holidays and if we were going to spend time with each other, at our own family's house or try to visit both sets of families. He had already met my parents so it was probably my turn to meet his. Also, I lived in the same town as my parents so I was

able to see them as often as I liked—a luxury he did not have with his own.

We planned the trip for me to meet his parents even with my reluctance. I started to remember the time he had his rash and contacted his mother before talking to me. I wondered what this woman thought of me and if she really wanted to meet me. Maybe she was just agreeing to this because she wanted to see her son and thought this may be the only way to see him over the holidays.

Dana was spending the day after Christmas through New Years with Mick again so she and I planned our travel arrangements together. I was so happy with the fact that I would be flying with someone versus having to travel alone with the "meeting the parents" anxiety. We decided to take the midnight flight because it was cheaper and we would get Christmas day/evening with our family then see our men and their families the very next day. Later we would discover that this was not such a good idea.

We landed at the airport really early in the morning—now I know why they call it the red eye. I definitely had red eyes for sure. When we got there we both dragged ourselves off of the flight that we were supposed to get some sleep on but didn't because most of the time was spent chatting. We met up with Mick and Peter and Mick told us that he and Dana were going to morning mass with his sister and her family. Dana asked Peter and I if we would go and we agreed. Another bad idea—because little did I know that shortly after mass I was heading over to Peter's parents house to meet them.

Dana and I giggled like little schoolgirls during mass because we were delirious from the lack of sleep our bodies were now enduring. I think Peter was getting a little bit frustrated at us because we were making noise. It was becoming obvious how serious he was about his religion and how anal retentive he really is. I guess Dana and I should have tried to get some sleep during mass . . . although we probably would have gotten in trouble doing that too. Now, looking like a sleep deprived raccoon, Peter and I headed over to his parents. The drive seemed like it took forever, which was only about forty-five minutes—again, another opportune time for sleep that I did not take advantage of.

We drove up to his parent's driveway and I had this horrible feeling in the pit of my stomach. I so hoped that the forgiveness factor embedded in the core of their religion would come in to play and his mom would conveniently forget about the supposed rash and the fact that I corrupted her virgin son. I mean it wasn't as if I had sacrificed an animal or something like that. Although if she wanted me to sacrifice an animal I am sure there are plenty out here in this rural small town.

I walked in the door and most of his immediate family members were there. I couldn't tell if they were looking at me in efforts of meeting me or just because I looked like death warmed over. I figured if they could like me when I looked like this then they would like me so much more when I actually looked like I got some rest. I felt very awkward with his family. They did seem nice when he introduced us but the only one that I felt somewhat comfortable with was his brother and his brother's family.

His sister was distant and uninterested in anything other than her life. She tended to her daughter as if her daughter was some sort of royalty. Everything her young daughter did was of great importance to her and she was not afraid to show how attached she was to her.

His mother was in the kitchen prepping our early dinner and seemed distracted as well. It seemed as if everyone but his brother was treating me as an intruder to their close nit family. I really felt like I have the words "rash and de-virginzed" written all over my forehead. Since I was staying at his parent's house for almost a week—in my own room without him I might add—I thought, "Wonderful, this is going to be the longest trip in the history of meeting someone's parents." Could my life get any better right now? Am I going to get any sleep in the near future? And, most importantly, do these people drink?

I set my bags in the room that was to be mine and tried to clean myself up before dinner. When I sat down at the dinner table I noticed that the only one that seemed to want to talk was his brother and his wife. His mother seemed like one of those old fashioned subservient mothers that did the kitchen duties but did not talk until spoken to—and, her responses when spoken to were brief at that. I wanted to be my normal goofy self but I feared that my lack of respect for the rules of engagement would take me out of the running for entry into this family. Was that what I really wanted—to be in a family that was apparently old fashioned in the sense that the woman takes care of the household duties while the men just ate at the dinner table practically grunting in between every bite.

After dinner Peter started reminiscing about his family and told me about one of the times he tried to teach his nephew a lesson.

"He was playing with the sink in my dad's workshop and he was told to stop playing around with it and didn't. So, without telling him when his face was close to the faucet I tuned it really high and it blasted into his face." He said.

"Wasn't he only around 8 years old?" I asked.

"Yes, that is what made it so funny." He said while laughing.

"He got water in his face and up his nose and then ran off crying. That is what he gets for not listening" He said.

I was in complete disarray. I thought to myself that that was horrible.

"Don't you think that was mean?" I asked in the calmest voice I could muster up.

"No, he shouldn't have been playing with the sink and that is what he gets."

Another shocker for me. Was I in the house of tricks and would something be done to me to teach me a lesson if I don't listen. God help me!

Over the week we did many things; we went for walks around the neighborhood, we took a ride on his parent's bikes, we even went into to town to sightsee. The awkwardness somewhat faded but had not left me completely. One night we wanted to get out of the house since we had been cooped up all day. We decided to head into town and go redeem some of the money from my Christmas Starbucks card. I was so excited since my favorite thing in the world is caffeine and my second favorite thing is Starbucks. We drove around and could not find a Starbucks to save our lives. Peter started to get frustrated because he did not feel it was necessary to spend over thirty minutes hunting down a coffee shop of any kind. All I could think to myself is that he could not understand my immeasurable love for those little brown, perfectly smelling and wonderfully tasting beans blended at this spectacular place. As he got more frustrated I noticed how immature he was being and I tried to laugh it off. Since we were near a grocery store he decided to stop there for a snack.

"We are going in there and finding something else or asking someone if a Starbucks is nearby." He said in a condescending tone as we approached the grocery store.

He then felt compelled to tell me, as if I was five years old, "And if there is no Starbucks around you better find something else or we are going home."

Wow I thought to myself. At what point did he see me as a five year old and why can't a grown adult be excited about coffee and using their Christmas gift card? Tis the season huh?

We went into the grocery store and he ran immediately for the ice cream isle. I slowly followed still feeling a little beaten down from the scolding in the car. His eyes became so huge and for one moment I thought I saw him tearing up.

"This ice cream is only local to this area and they are the only ice cream company that makes my favorite flavor, Banana Pudding. I have not had this flavor in years" he said.

Well, the flavor that he found sounded really horrible to me but I wasn't going to ruin his Christmas high like he did mine.

"Well, I don't think I would like that flavor so why don't we get two separate flavors of ice cream so we both can have what we want and forget about Starbucks." I said calmly so I wouldn't lose out on another opportunity to enjoy something sweet for Christmas.

"I like bananas and I like pudding but I prefer to keep them separate." I said hoping he would compromise.

I thought for sure this would be a win-win to this Christmas dilemma. Wrong again. He proceeded to look at the price of both containers of ice cream and said,

"I don't want to pay that much for ice cream and you are the only one that will eat your flavor. Your container will just sit at my house until it is thrown away and that would be a waste of money."

Is it not Christmas after all? I mean, if we cannot splurge a little during the holidays then when can we splurge? And, this was getting him off of the Survivor's race to Starbucks.

"What will I have then if we don't get any ice cream for me and we don't go to Starbucks?"

"You can have some of mine or the cookies you liked back at my mom's."

"Do you think that it fair that you are the only one getting anything from this road trip?" I asked not sure if I want to poke the bear so to speak.

"I want this ice cream, this is my favorite ice cream and I want it." He said in a whining tone.

He basically threw an adult size child fit in the grocery store. In order to avoid embarrassment I said ok let's get your ice cream and go. All of a sudden his mood changed from grumpy to excited and he started to hug me and kiss me on my cheek.

After the purchase—*for him I might add*—we got into the car and started driving back to his parent's house. I was quiet for a few minutes trying to process what just happened in the grocery store and understand how his mood could change that quickly.

"What is wrong?" He asked me in a somewhat frustrated tone.

"Nothing." I said

I was afraid to say anything thinking that Dr. Jekyll would turn into Mr. Hyde again with no notice. After being quiet for a few more minutes he became agitated.

"Is this what you are going to do all night? Are you going to pout and not talk to me?"

Before I had a chance to answer, thinking of the best course of action, he started raising his voice saying that we will find a Starbucks if it takes all night.

I still did not say anything afraid that it would worsen the situation. Luckily, we stumbled across the coffee shop within only a couple of minutes from his severe mood change. I went in and got my goodies and returned to the car. He was upset because his precious ice cream was melting and it wasn't going to be the same when he gets home to eat it. About this time into the trip I was glad we had separate bedrooms. I needed some space and wanted to think about what had happened and if this was who he really was or maybe the stress from the trip was seeping out a bit. Regardless, I needed to determine if this would be consistent behavior because I do not think I could date or spend my life with someone that was this selfish and immature.

One day we decided to go to the local gym together. On the way there his phone rang. He looked to see who it was and let it go to voicemail.

"Do you need to take that?" I asked when we arrived at the gym.

"No." he said.

"Since we are running a little late and we were supposed to go to your sisters for dinner was that her?" I asked hoping he would give me some hint as to who it was without having to pry.

"No, it wasn't my sister it was Jessabel. I will call her back later." He said.

I could not help but wonder who this woman was and why he never talked to her in front of me. Did she even know I existed? Was she trying to impede on my territory? I guess I'll work out all of this curiosity in the gym.

Over the course of the week I noticed that his parents really never spent much time together. They were retired and had tons of hobbies but none that seemed to overlap. His mother was in her garden a lot while the dad was in his workshop most of the time. The only time I saw them together was when we ate meals and at the end of the night when they retired for bed. The odd thing about his parents was that they rarely spoke to each other. It seemed that their conversations were limited to one or two sentences and then they would move one to their next hobby or task. Is this how married-retired couples are after spending twenty plus years together? Is this what I had to look forward to? I couldn't imagine that Peter would end up like this especially since we talked for hours on the phone most nights.

One day when his parents were busy doing their separate activities we decided to take a long walk before dinner. While we were on the walk Peter's phone rang and guess who it was? Jessabel was calling again. He let it go to voicemail and I was fed up with this so-called friend that kept calling.

"What did she say when she left a voicemail?" I asked.

"She said she has rats in her basement and she wants to know how to get rid of them." He said.

"Doesn't she know you are on a trip with me trying to spend time with your family?" I asked somewhat frustrated.

"I think so." He said.

"Well, I think it's pretty rude to call you repeatedly when she doesn't even know me or try to get to know me for that matter. You should call her back and let her know where you are and that you are trying to spend time with your family." I said.

"I will call her later." He said.

"No, I think you should call her now, unless you are hiding something and there is a reason why you can't talk to her in front of me." I said.

"No, there isn't so I will call her back." He said.

That plan didn't work out as well as I thought it would. I figured she would find out that he was spending time with me and have respect for that and say hi and that would be it. But, it didn't work out so nicely. She never said hi to me and apologized for calling him, playing the victim, so he got upset with me for making her feel bad. No mention as to how it made me feel that he had been so secretive about her all this time. I was the bad guy again.

We ended up arguing about it on the walk back to him parents house. We didn't talk much during dinner so we fit right in with the crowd. Then, after dinner he went off to do something in his room and I went outside to sit on their porch swing in the back. I must have been out there for about an hour and yet no one came out to check on me in the dark not even Peter.

When am I leaving to go back home?

CHAPTER 8

Holy mackerel

Now back at home and back to our routines we somehow got past the time spent at his parent's

house—which seemed like one of those foreign hostels as distant as everyone was. The only difference was that most hostels would have foreigners trying to get to know each other so there would most likely be more conversation. As time moved on it seemed as if we were becoming more and more serious. I do not know if we were cutting the incidents slack because of the long distance involved or the fact that this was his first real relationship but somehow we were moving forward. We started talking more and more about the long term and wondering if our values and beliefs would match

that of the others. We started talking about a biggie—religion.

He was born and raised Catholic and I was not baptized at birth because my mother decided to leave religion up to both my sister and me. I think many of my mother's decisions regarding religion were based from her bitterness towards the fact that her mother died at a young age and after our dad leaving when my sister I were both very young never to return. I think she somehow wondered how either of those events could happen if there was really a God. Or, maybe she prayed for both situations with no results leaving her to wonder if praying was worth it. I always wondered as a child what it would have been like to believe in a higher power. I did believe in God but never really had any support in that belief or had the opportunity to learn more. I decided that I wanted my children to have a religion from birth even if they wanted something else later in life. I at least wanted them to have something to believe in and have a place to go every Sunday to hear the readings and be exposed to the positive reinforcements.

Peter and I talked about it in great lengths and I decided to go to Catholic classes also known as RCIA.

"I do not want to live with anyone who does not share the same religious belief as I do." Peter said.

"I have had many friends that were Catholic and have been to mass many times. I like the atmosphere and most of my beliefs are consistent with what Catholicism offers." I said.

"I am excited for you to take the classes." He said.

"I just hope you help me learn some of the information if I need help." I said.

"Of course." He said.

He was very adamant that he would certainly not marry anyone without them being Catholic. I started to search around town for a Catholic church offering these classes for less than a two year period and found only one. Most of the churches wanted you to attend their classes for at least two years. Well, I didn't have that kind of time. Peter and I were already at the one year mark and that meant at least one more year apart at the very least. Neither one of us wanted the long distance relationship to remain long distance any longer than it needed. It was a struggle for both of us.

I finally enrolled in the classes feeling pretty awkward and unfamiliar with the place. I had been to Mass before but never had I gone by myself or signed myself up for such a commitment. I feared that God would see me coming and somehow lose my enrollment paperwork. I did have some issues after all. I de-virginized a seemingly innocent Catholic man and was having pre-marital sex.

I went to the RCIA classes not knowing much about Catholicism and the people in the class. Most people were really nice so I wondered why my mother never wanted to come to a place like this. Church was free and everyone seemed so pleasant—maybe this is just day one of class and things will change as time moves forward. I just hope that lightning somehow doesn't transcend downward though the ceiling and accidently land on my head—accidently being the key word. I felt awkward being there by myself and really wanted to have Peter's support throughout this process.

I learned a lot over the several months of RCIA classes. I tried to memorize everything they covered each night. I figured I had a lot of making up to do since most Catholics I knew had their whole life to learn about the religion. If I was going to carry on an educated conversation with Peter I better make sure I have my facts straight. One thing that bothered me most was seeing everyone with their spouses or spouses to be. I was alone trying to bond with whoever sat at my table each night. Most nights I felt really alone and wondered if I was doing this for myself or for the hopes that Peter would find me acceptable after I was baptized for the very first time in my life.

All of my sins would soon be forgiven at the time of the baptism. Should I go out and make some more mistakes before then to get it all forgiven in one shot? No, that is just my non-religious side talking. I am now moving on to greener pastures and becoming closer to the Lord—Hallelujah!

A couple of nights I called Peter after class because I was so excited about my accomplishment I wanted to share what I had learned and I forgot he was three hours ahead and woke him up. One night I called him upset because I wanted this process to be something I actually shared with someone but I was alone every night except for my classmates—and the Lord. When I called him upset he was cranky because he was tired and pretty much shut me down and made me feel like I was overreacting and should not be upset.

"Hello?" he said in a very tired cranky voice.

"Hey, I just wanted to tell you how my night went at class." I said

"Yeah, do you know what time it is?" He said in a tone that implied I should get the hint and let him go.

"I am really sad because I have been going through these classes by myself for quite a while and everyone has someone else to share it with. I really miss you and I feel really sad that you cannot be here with me." I said almost in tears.

"I need to get up for work early, I have to go." He said.

"You cannot talk for just a few minutes?" I asked in the hopes that he would somewhat put my mind at ease and remind me that he was proud of me or give me some kind of support of any kind."

"It's late I have to go." He said.

"Ok." I said in a somewhat quivering voice trying not to cry.

"Bye." He said and then hung up before I had a chance to say goodbye back.

I was still in the parking lot and I broke down crying. Luckily everyone had pretty much left and it was dark so if anyone was still there they probably wouldn't be able to see me. It was just as lonely in the parking lot as in the classes. I felt bad for seeming like a burden and then for waking him up. Am I not supposed to have feelings of any kind? I wasn't sure exactly how I should have been feeling at that moment. I couldn't believe that he did not understand my feelings of loneliness.

The day came when there was a church event to go to and Peter said he would fly out to be there with me. When we were on the phone somehow Jessabel came up again. I found out that she asked him recently to go and watch her play volleyball. Call me crazy but I think this woman likes my man.

"Don't you think she is trying to spend a lot of time with you?" I asked.

"No, she just wants to be friends." He said.

"I am not entirely sure that is all she has intended." I said.

"I can't believe you are reading more into this that there is." He said.

"I can't believe that you don't see the signs and why doesn't she find someone else to hang out with all of these times?" I said.

"I don't want to talk about it anymore." He said.

I let it go for now and figured I would wait to see how many more attempts she would make to spend time with him.

Peter flew out for the church ceremony and all was well, so much so that we sang and held hands at church. Then, one song played that sounded like it had the same tune as a Beethoven song. I leaned over to quietly tell him this and he looked at me and said, "shhhh." He seemed irritated. I couldn't believe that he was being rude like that. I decided to sing and smile like it didn't even bother me—until we got into the car.

I tried to tell him what I was trying to say in church and he shut me down again.

"That was not the tune of a Beethoven song and I have no idea what you are talking about." He said in a smug tone.

"Yes it was and what is the big deal." I said.

I could not believe he was so insistent on being right.

"Do you want to bet on it?" I said in a playful way.

"I don't need to bet on it because I am right." He said in a very cocky tone.

I became very frustrated and was getting really tired of his attitude. He was being arrogant and it came across so demeaning that I just had to call him out on it.

Well, calling him on it just made matters worse. He denied acting like a smug know-it-all and the fight began. Wow, I just went through this major connection with the church and God and now my boyfriend and I are fighting over Beethoven. I guess it is a good thing Beethoven couldn't hear because if he were alive he would be utterly disgusted by our behavior and my boyfriend's apparent ignorance in regards to classical music.

In his defense he did have a Bachelors degree in Chemical Engineering and he was pursuing an MBA from a very prestigious university. It sure sounds to me like he should be well versed in classical music from the plethora of knowledge acquired at said institutions. Maybe this is me being a little sarcastic but it was all I could do to stop myself from driving clear across town to purchase a DVD in efforts of proving him wrong. And, boy what a pleasure that would have been—so I waited until we got home and I looked it up on the Internet.

Then, when the proof was right in front of his face, he finally acknowledged for a very brief moment that there was some resemblance and went on like nothing had happened. Was I in the twilight zone? Fights would start over the littlest things and then he would act as if the fight never happened a mere twenty minutes later without even talking about it. I guess I should count my blessing that the fight did not drag on since he was only out for a short period of time.

After he left and went back home I started to wonder where we were going with the relationship and if we were really resolving any of the random issues that popped up and then only to shortly thereafter dismiss. Since I was busy working full time and taking the RCIA classes I tried to calm my wandering mind and let God handle it for the meantime.

The day came to get baptized and he was there as he promised he would be. Is there another Beethoven song dispute on the horizon? This day was pretty special to both of us especially since this process was a year in the making. I was grateful that all of my sins were soon to be erased. It turned out that there were no debates about any of the tunes played during church so all was well.

This was a major accomplishment in my life and I felt as if I made the right decision. I had gotten to know some of the people in the class and became close with my sponsor. My sponsor even invited Peter and I out to breakfast when Peter was in town during the baptism. It appeared like it was all coming together. Peter and my sponsor really hit it off. It seemed like my sponsor thought he was a pretty decent guy. That made me feel so much better considering some of my recent doubts about fights that would dissolve without any in-depth conversation or true resolution.

This was another weekend that came and went all too fast. I was now Catholic and Peter and I were seeing each other every three to four months. Was the long distance thing really that bad after all? I think he was now ready for me to move in with him. Would I really want to move to the Midwest and leave my family? Is it time for me to start my life somewhere else and will it work out for the best?

CHAPTER 9

Moving in together

The day finally approached when he talked me into moving out to the cold Midwest. I stalled as long as I could have trying to ensure that I would not be moving during the ice cold winter months. We planned everything down to the minute detail. He was the biggest planner I knew. He had lists for everything including every aspect of the move. When he came out to help me pack the moving truck he seemed very happy and excited. We made such a great moving team. We took direction from each other without conflict and even when we were both getting tired we remained respectful to each other and did not let it ruin the excitement.

I hoped that the minor issues we had prior were the worst of it especially now that I decided to uproot my two cats and head out almost to the other side of the United States. We had everything packed and I said my goodbyes—wow, was that hard. My mom and I cried and even my step dad seemed teary eyed at goodbye.

The new found confidence of my relationship with Peter helped me get into the car and get to the airport. When we got to the airport we found it packed with people. I had two sedated cats and Peter and I were exhausted from packing the moving truck. We sat and waited while our flight got delayed and delayed and then eventually we were told that we missed our connecting flight.

After only 10 hours of waiting in the wonderfully entertaining airport we flew to our layover destination. The airport put us up in a hotel only to get up again at the crack of dawn the next day to try it all over again. At least we were almost half way there. My cats were not happy to say the least. They meowed all night in the hotel room while we tried to sleep.

The next morning we made it to the airport and made it onto our flight—and on time go figure. Unfortunately the cats had to be sedated again which really should have been us because of the stress. We looked like death warmed over. We were both exhausted from spending so much time traveling. Was this ordeal a sign that I shouldn't be moving in with him? Or, was it a test to see how determined we both would be to make it happen. I guess time will tell.

We made it to his house, unpacked and started our journey of living together. The first few days seemed just like our normal trips but then it got weird—very weird. I wasn't working yet so I started to do things around the house in attempts of earning my keeps as some would say. I thought I should do something while I was home and he was working. In between looking for jobs I cleaned the house and made sure dinner was always waiting for him.

Boy was I in for a shocker. When he got home one day I got a lecture on how the cord on the vacuum was not put back correctly. Another day I discovered that I folded his clothes incorrectly so I received an official lesson on that. He was kind enough to fold them in front of me plenty of times so I wouldn't make that horrific mistake again. We even had a debate about whether to use a sponge or a dish rag when cleaning the dishes. Apparently he had always used a rag, which I am sure he learned from his mother. I used a sponge, and since I cleaned the dishes regularly I thought it would be alright to use said sponge.

After a mild argument regarding the sponge vs. dish rag somehow we compromised and said that both could be used depending on who was doing the dishes. I think he would offer to do the dishes just because of this debate and to try to irritate me by using the rag. Isn't life too short to be having these disagreements over something so petty? Did I just move in with that guy from Sleeping with the Enemy?

Out of the blue I asked him when he last spoke with Jessabel and he said that they don't talk anymore. I wondered if he was just saying that or if he stopped talking to her because she did indeed like him and it would have been evident if I met her.

The incident that really took the cake was his obsession with me not using the same spoon for the peanut butter and the jelly. He would not budge on this one at all. He said that it is not sterile to mix them. Was he a doctor—o' wait no he wasn't. Didn't we learn this lesson all too well when he tried to self-diagnose his supposed STD rash from before? I had been using the same spoon and double dipping for years and I was still alive. Maybe that meant I could survive in the harshest conditions. Hopefully it meant I could survive in this condition.

"What would you do if I forgot and accidently used the same spoon for both without washing the spoon in between? I asked.

"Then we would have a discussion as to why you are forgetting so we can work together to make sure it didn't happen again." He said in a very serious tone.

Wow—was all I could think when my mind wandered off thinking about the bathroom towels— were they folded correctly and leveled off, was the bed made with everything level and all of the bumps pushed out, did I vacuum around the edges of the floor in the event that he would bust out his CSI kit and look for some DNA? O' wait are we having an actual conversation about this and I should I look like I am interested? The nice thing was that he was done with his lecture at the exact same time my daydreaming ended. What a coincidence. Now I know how men tune out women and why for that matter.

I tried to give him a hug and kiss afterwards to somewhat diffuse the slightly tense situation and in hopes that he would show me that he appreciated my efforts in the slightest when he dodged my affection and laughed. He did this a few times. After repeated attempts I gave up and went upstairs to be by myself— again!

I was beginning to worry each day as I found another oddity about the man I decided to move all the way across the United States for. I wondered if some of these things could be changed or if he could tone it down a bit. Each day I discovered that he really could not tone any of it down. He was compelled to maintain control over his life and apparently mine regardless of what input I had.

Most of his belongings were from his earlier years. He had this hideous lamp that his mother gave him in high school that looked like a huge tree stump from afar. When closing in on this hideous item posing for a lamp you actually discover another wonder—there is a built in coaster stemming off of the trunk like base that holds the light bulb in place. He said it had sentimental value and that is why he kept it so long. His mother was still alive so I wasn't sure why it had that much value. Soon thereafter I found out most of his things had great value and that he would later have an agonizing time letting anything go.

In order to justify the strange phenomenon of keeping everything (even down to the matches and wine corks) he told me how his dad always made the children squish the last tiny piece of soap into a new bar soap so no soap was wasted. Yet another thing to add to my list of things to do. He wasn't so persistent on this one but he did try to encourage me to squeegee the shower doors every time I took a shower. Who has time for all of this? I can barely remember what I need to do in my life and now I have to add all of his pet peeves to that same list. Will I have time to breathe? Or will that too be done to his standards?

One day he came rushing in from work telling me there was this nice bench on the side of the road that someone was getting rid of and it was free. I wasn't sure if he was more excited by the bench or the fact that it was free.

"Hurry, let's go get it." He said excitedly.

"Ok, what does it look like?" I asked.

"It is a nice teak bench that we can sand down and stain to put in the back yard. This could be a couple's project that we work on together."

We got the bench and carried it almost 2 blocks to the house in what seemed like 90 degree weather with humidity that was off the charts and put it in the basement. He needed to check to see if we had the right supplies to work on it so we left the project for another day.

We had one date night a week because of his frugalness and his inability to pay for overpriced one-time only meals. Often when the check would come at a restaurant he would tell me how expensive I was no matter how cheap the check was and I would hear more stories about how his dad would never pay for meals outside of the house. Sometimes he would smirk when saying it but I got the message. It was painstaking for him to part with his precious money even if it was an attempt to be romantic.

Date nights were slowly becoming a chore. I felt like I had to do them for the sake of our relationship but only to be left feeling like a burden. Each month that went on that I didn't have a full time job I felt even more like a burden. One day he came home and I had been so discouraged from not getting any interviews I broke down and cried.

"I am so sorry that I am still not working and I am trying to do everything else to help like cleaning, cooking, and running errands." I said.

I even showed him my spreadsheet that I had of all of the places I applied to which totaled over 80 places.

"I think I am going to start cleaning houses on the side since I like cleaning so much." I said slightly hopeful.

"It is ok Honey; you will get a job soon." He said while hugging me."

Not only did I feel like a financial burden and a failure at the chores I also started to notice that we barely talked when we were together let alone on the phone while he is as work. I confronted him about this and he got angry.

"Do you notice that we don't talk that much anymore?" I said.

"I am busy and we see each other at home every day that should be enough." He said in an irritated tone.

Sadly though, the date nights were pretty much the only time we spent together throughout the week that exceeded 20 minutes—unless we were running errands on the weekend together. He went cycling a couple of times a week and then most other nights he was on his computer for hours at a time. I knew that we wouldn't spend several hours on the phone like we used to but we were pretty distant for two people living together trying to maintain a relationship.

I was starting to see the similarities between our situation and that of his parents. The woman cleans, cooks, and takes care of anything else that is, for lack of a better phrase, "women's work" and the man takes care of the finances, the workshop, and anything else deemed to be "man's work." I was starting to get really lonely.

One day when I was spending time with one of my friends they asked me what was wrong and I said, "I feel like Peter and I don't spend time together anymore and I feel as if we dedicated more time to our relationship when we lived in separate states." My friend said, "Relationships are like plants, if you don't water them they eventually dry up and die." That was encouraging! Peter watered his plants on a regular basis and they were even on his to-do list. Where did I rank; or did I? How do I get on his to-do list?

I tried to find hobbies we could do together and I found out that he liked to do woodworking—that was out for me. We both liked to run and we both liked to read. I would have gone cycling with him but I couldn't cycle fast enough for his standards. I started waking up every early day to go running trying to increase my speed and build up my endurance. I even suggested us getting into bed earlier so we can read together. Well, I could never run fast enough nor could we get to bed early enough to read together.

It almost seemed like he wanted his life exactly as it was before me. How would I fit in and how are we going to overcome this significant change for both of us? What about what I wanted to do? Does he really have to run like a bullet every time we go running? Does he really have to cycle at cheetah speed?

Several days went by and we hadn't really seen much of each other or talked. So, one day when he was home I heard him laughing upstairs in the office. I went to sit on the stairs so I could hear his voice and hear him laugh. I was pretty lonely since I only had a few friends and I missed my family so much. It was nice to hear him laugh—I missed that from our phone calls when we were dating.

Then, after a couple of minutes of listening I couldn't believe what I was hearing. He was saying things like, "she has so many bills, and she can't even get a job." I could not believe what I was hearing. He went on to talk about how much of a financial burden I was and that he didn't want to be responsible for my debt. He was afraid that he might have to stop contributing to one of his IRA accounts and lower the investment amount for his 401k (which was already at the maximum contribution).

All I kept thinking was that if he was so afraid of the financial obligation then why did he have me move out here before I had a job? I was doing the best I could do to look for a full time job. I guess this was not good enough. The house was immaculate and dinner was always done precisely when he walked through the door. Anything that needed to be done at home that I could do I did. Why didn't he come to me if this was such a problem and who is he telling this to?

I later found out that he had this same type of discussion with his good friend Trevor who lived in the area, his mother, his father, his sister, and God knows who else. I was crushed. I felt like our relationship was taking a toll that would be close to impossible to overcome.

Somehow later he convinced me that it wasn't as bad as I heard and that he was just afraid of the financial obligation because he was used to only paying for himself. He said things would be ok. I doubted it and now tried even harder than ever to get a job in the event that I would need to take care of myself one hundred percent.

There was a retail store I frequented when I actually had a full time job that might be hiring. I visited the store and the manager there took to me right away. She started talking to me and said that I should do sales because I had such an outgoing personality. I had no idea what I could or wanted to do. I was open for anything even being a cashier. I just wanted something that would provide a paycheck. I wondered if this job would be good enough for Peter or if he would be ashamed to be dating someone working for less than what he believed to be an acceptable pay rate. At this point, money is money and I needed a job. I filled out my application and they hired me shortly thereafter.

I was trained by one of the best saleswomen they had. Lenora, my trainer and co-worker taught me all of the ropes. She worked with me side by side and showed me how she helps everyone regardless of their personality or needs. Lenora was impressive—she moved fast and was so helpful and pleasant to everyone. She inspired me to be an awesome saleswoman. I loved my job even though I didn't make very much money. Every day I actually looked forward to going to work and seeing all of the people that would come in and my co-workers.

This job was the only thing that took my mind off of my distressed life. I used this job to survive the emotional weight bearing down on me when I was with Peter and while I tried to look for a full time job. There was one co-worker I just fell in love with, as a friend of course. His name was Jonah and he was one of the funniest people working there. He and I hit it off so much it was as if we knew each other from before. He knew I was with Peter and he respected that. He was a breath of fresh air for me. Every time we saw each other we laughed so much. I couldn't believe that I could be that happy in my current situation. We started hanging out after work and even when Peter found out how much time we spent together he didn't care. He said that he trusted me and it didn't bother him. Personally I think he preferred it because then he would have more time for his hobbies and himself when I wasn't around. It was somewhat of a win-win for both of us ~ sort of. It seemed really sad to me that the man I lived with was not the man I wanted to spend all of my time with because it was Jonah.

One of my days off Jonah and I went to play pool at the pool hall down the street and we were the only two there. We had such a good time. I even had a couple of drinks since I didn't have to work. I got a call from Peter while we were there and I just let the phone ring until it went to voicemail. I was somewhat buzzed by my drink and thought it was funny that finally the tables turned. I was the one busy when he wanted to talk to me. And, I was not going to let him ruin the time I was having by saying some snide comment about me not working while he was. This day was one day I didn't want to ruin because it was so nice to forget about my job search, my cleaning, and my financial burdens. When we were at the pool haul Jonah said to me,

"You know Peter doesn't appreciate you at all for what you are worth. If it was me I would want to spend every minute I could with you."

I couldn't stop from thinking about how this is the way it is supposed to be with couples. Maybe not every minute a day twenty four hours a day but at least as much time as possible. I did not have that in my relationship. I made up some excuse for the way our relationship was, like he is very busy or he is still getting used to having me around or a relationship in general. I was saying anything I could think of regarding my situation so I wouldn't have to see it as it really was.

Sometimes when I got off early at work because they were slow and cutting hours I would stay out if I knew Peter was home because if I came home I knew I would just bother him. Most times I would hang out at the bookstore by myself and read. It was sad to feel as if I couldn't go to my own home. But then again it didn't even seem like my home, it seemed like the place I was staying that he was paying for.

The distance continued to grow as time flew by and fights were now becoming weekly. One of our biggest fights was on a Sunday—the Holy day. Peter wanted to go to mass early and I was tired from working the night before—not to mention I was not a morning person which he knew. He got up, got in the shower and got ready for church while I was still in bed.

"Where are you going?" I asked him.

"Church." He said.

"Don't you want to go together when we can actually both go?" I said.

"I want to go now!" He said, in a very spoiled brat kind of way,

I started to get upset because this was yet another thing he was doing without me. It seemed like he didn't care if we were together at all anymore. If I was ready when he wanted to go somewhere I could go but only if I wanted to go where he wanted and when he wanted to go. He got really mad that I was upset blaming me that I was trying to make him feel bad and that his needs were not being met because he needed to go to church early. What? Things got so overdramatized.

"If you want to go with me then you can come." He said in yet another irritated tone.

By that time I was crying and I didn't have anything picked out to wear for church.

"I will have to go like this." I said

Getting even more irritated he said, "Fine, let's just go."

Out the door we went with me in jeans and a somewhat nice sweater—trying to stop crying I might add. While we were driving he got so angry that I would not stop crying before church he slammed on the brakes and pulled over in a parking lot.

"I am not going to go in with you crying." He said snapping at me.

Did he try to make me feel better? No. Did he say any encouraging words like I am glad that you tried to come? No.

"I am taking you home." He yelled.

I was so upset and confused I jumped out of the car and started walking. He jumped out of the car too and started yelling at me in front of people walking down the street. I was crying and he was yelling—it was a beautiful sight. This would have been a great time for tourists to come and photograph something. We were the epitome of good relationships in the Midwest.

Finally I walked away from him and he stomped away from me in the direction of church. A few minutes went by and he came running over to me.

"I don't want it to be like this." He said.

What was this—Dr. Jekyll and Mr. Hyde again? I was so tired of giving in that I said, "Just forget it." And he gave up quicker than a bloody leg getting massacred in a pool of hungry piranhas. I guess he went to church because when I turned around all I saw were the heels of his feet as he ran in that direction.

We didn't make up for several days after that. The mornings he ignored me I found him giddily signing songs that he deemed theme appropriate to mock me when I passed him in the hallway. He said he didn't like fighting but when we disagreed he did things that would result in a nasty fight. He always pretended to be so happy, humming, singing and whistling after a fight as if it didn't faze him a bit that we weren't talking.

Is this really normal behavior? And, how much of this should I overlook because this was his first relationship after all? It's almost as if he looked forward to the fights because then he could do all of his hobbies with absolutely no guilt whatsoever. At least, that is what he thought. There would be consequence later. He just didn't realize how much of a toll this was taking on us.

My patience was diminishing as I felt my personality slowly drifting away. I felt as if nothing was good enough for him. I couldn't get a full time job, everything that I cleaned was done incorrectly, and I wanted too much of his time even though I only asked for a few hours a week. Was the delay at the airport a sign that I should have never gotten on that flight with my two cats? How can he expect his life to remain the same when he now has someone in it? Most importantly, how could he say those derogatory things about me to his family and friends? I guess if you focus so much on the negative you will eventually believe things are worse than they are if you tell yourself so. Maybe he was brainwashing himself to think he had it worse than he did. Maybe I was brainwashing myself to think that I had it better than I did.

CHAPTER 10

As good as it gets

Finally I got a full time job. I was on cloud nine thinking that this would help our exhausted relationship. Hopefully I could contribute financially

like he wanted me to all along. It was a great job—not as much money as I had hoped for but there was a great deal of opportunities once you got your foot in the door. I called Peter to tell him that I was offered the job and he was excited for me. I really felt that this was it for us. We were finally getting the reprieve we needed for quite some time.

We went out to dinner and celebrated. He was still frugal with the bill because he said I hadn't received a pay check yet so we shouldn't spend money we didn't have. I just wanted to celebrate within reason—I didn't want to worry about the money. Maybe one night in our future he won't remind me how much is spent on dinner.

Then later that week he asked to see my offer letter. I thought that was odd. I asked him why and he said that he hadn't seen an offer letter in a while. That was the first lie of many he would tell me as the days progressed. It is amazing how your instincts kick in when something isn't quite right. I showed him the letter and he read it thoroughly. Maybe that was all I thought—nothing else to it. Then, it started adding up in my head. We hadn't spent much time together in quite some time, every time he talked about our relationship it was so horrible in his mind like nothing ever changed even though it did, his derogatory comments about me on the phone and anything else I was missing. Something wasn't right. It was starting to feel like a really bad after school special. Where was the unmarked van and the man with candy?

Sunday came and he was off to church as usual. I made an excuse not to go. I wasn't feeling like spending anytime with him right now until I figure things out. I went upstairs to the office and got on the computer. I thought that maybe some internet surfing would take my mind off of things when I noticed a manila folder on the desk. Something kept telling me to open it. I had never gone through any of his things before. My belief was that if I didn't trust him I shouldn't be with him. But that folder kept staring at me practically begging me to open it. I opened it and at first found nothing but papers about a trip he took for work that he said was for training.

My stomach was still nervous for some strange reason when I found something. It was an interview he went to. There was no training. And the interview was for a job in New York. My stomach sank and I started to feel nauseas. I called my mom and talked to her frantically while she tried to reassure me by saying that maybe he wanted me to go with him.

He had one of his infamous lists made in this stack of paperwork that indicated what furniture he needed for his new place and one of them was a couch. I had a couch and we had a couch now that we lived together. He especially liked my couch because he didn't have one when we met and mine was free. That told me right there that he was trying to get away and that is why he wanted to see my offer letter. He wanted to make sure I had a job so he could leave.

I was trying to pull myself together before he got home. When he came home I asked him how church was and he said, "Great." Of course church is great but what about us is what I thought. I asked him to sit down because I wanted to talk to him about a couple of things. He didn't look too interested. He acted like he had better things to do but sat down anyway. I asked him about our relationship and asked if he felt that we were doing ok and he said, "We have some things to work out, why?"

"How long do you think we will be together?" I asked.

He started to get agitated kind of like a hungry lion in its cage after it has been poked with a stick a few times. Eventually things escalated and I called him out on what I found in the infamous manila folder—that damn folder. Will I ever be able to use manila folders again or will I be forced to use colored ones in order to keep this awful memory suppressed in my mind forever?

"I saw what was in your folder upstairs." I said

"What were you doing going through my stuff?" he said.

"That doesn't matter now. I know that you had a job interview in New York." I said.

"Yeah" he said.

"Were you going to tell me or were you just going to leave me here knowing I can't pay the bills?"

"I don't know." He said.

"So, you don't know if you were going to move out, take all of your stuff, and just be gone one day while I was at work?" I said

"I don't know I didn't get that far." He said.

Basically, the breakdown of what was in the folder was his sad pathetic attempt to get a job in New York and leave one day—apparently without telling me. The irony about all of this is it came right after we happily celebrated his birthday in which I took him out to an expensive dinner that he had no problem eating, I bought him a nice wallet that I got for a really good price and a nice pair of his favorite running shoes. And, after us celebrating my new job that took me several blood, sweat, and tear filled months to get. The gifts were all of which I did not have the money for but I really wanted him to see how nice it is to do something special for someone you care about.

He accepted the gifts without hesitation knowing that I hadn't made a dime yet. I guess after paying the grocery bill all of those months he felt he earned these gifts even after lecturing me about buying fruit that isn't on sale and how I better eat all of it or else. Grocery shopping was much like our date night—obsessions about spending an inordinate amount of money on food while the experience loses the fight to the paranoid schizophrenic thought that an extra pear will break the bank. What it actually breaks down to is two dollars less in his investment accounts. My mistake was that I bought him these things before I actually got a paycheck. I figured I could pay it off once I made some money. I had no idea I would be stranded in the middle of the United States to fend for myself because some schmuck of a guy wanted to just disappear one day.

CHAPTER 11

The Big Apple

The damage was done. Months of fighting, words said damning the other, excessive time spent apart, intimacy lost well after my eggs had left the building and were well hidden in witness protection. The feeling of having your entire world turned upside down was absolutely overwhelming.

I had come to love the Midwest and its' welcome to me. I had made several friends and adjusted to being without my family for the first time in my life. I looked at him while we were fighting about the contents of the manila folder and I said, "Send me home now!" He tried to talk to me about staying for my job saying that we could be friends. I looked at him like he was crazy. After going back and forth I said, "What is wrong with you, how could you treat me this way?" I asked,

"You mess with people like your nephew with the water and me when I try to give you affection and you dodge my affection like it is a game." I said.

He stood there with a shocked look on his face as if this was acceptable behavior on his behalf. At one point he looked at me as tears were forming in his eyes and said,

"I don't know what is wrong with me, I like messing with people until they crack."

All I thought to myself is get me out of here and God I cannot believe I moved all of the way out here for this sick bastard. Was he doing all of these mean things deliberately? Next, someone is going to find my body in the basement all chopped up—but in really nice consistently shaped and sized pieces as I don't think he would have it any other way. Were his actions all this time deliberant?

When things calmed down we both called our parents and broke the news. His parents were grateful because he was after all living in sin. In fact at one point in our non-joint/non-marital venture his dad turned off the internet service that they were both sharing when he found out I was on it because I was living with him without his father's knowledge. What a great way for his parents to find that out. That should have been a sign that something wasn't right. He should have been proud that we were living together and he should have stood up to his parents.

This was just one of the many disappointments I experienced over the duration of what some call a relationship but what I call cohabitation and his parents would so lovely refer to as living in sin. His dad went on to say over the phone—which I could hear because I was sitting right next to him on the couch, "Don't have sex with her she might get pregnant and you don't need that and don't pay for anything because it was her decision to come out there." Now I really felt like I was going to throw up. I am beginning to see where Peter got his dysfunctional behavior from—his generous caring father. I am also seeing why his mother doesn't spend much time with the man—he is a rude, unsympathetic nut case.

My mom was telling me not to listen to what she called his pathetic parents. She said, "That is horrible to say about someone that loved their son and how can they be good people to allow their son to leave you stranded without any help when you just got a job." My mom was livid to say the least. She went on to say that that is probably why he is who he is, because of his parent's negative influence. She said that if that is how they treat people then sadly he doesn't know any better but that doesn't mean I have to put up with it. She was right yet again! I needed to get out of there and fast.

He bought me a ticket and I flew home the next day. On the plane, I sat in the seat next to the window staring out at the clouds and blue sky with tears streaming down my face while I watched the Midwest get smaller and smaller. My heart was breaking and I wondered how I would get the strength to make it through what was to come.

CHAPTER 12

Only the lonely

The next few weeks while I was back at home dragged on so much so that I felt like I was one hundred and twenty years old waiting finally for my time to come. I really felt that exhausted and hopeless. I knew our relationship was decaying but I never thought he would treat me the way he did and betray me that way. I always hoped that if we didn't make it we would at the very least try to be civil and help each other get a place of our own and be honest with each other. He was famously known for being dishonest from the beginning. Is this what he considers a trust worthy person? Is almost being abandoned worse than being cheated on? I'm not sure which one would have left a bigger hole.

I rarely ate; I showered at best once a week, my mom commonly found me in random rooms staring off into the distance. She wanted me to run errands with her but going to the grocery store was like a punishment with all of the memories of trying to calculate the cheapest fruit, trying to justify why I want the fruit that is not on sale. When my mom said, "get whatever fruit you want regardless of the price", I would tear up because her act of kindness what something I hadn't felt for some time.

He didn't even pay for my ticket back out there to get my things. I guess he felt as if it was someone else's responsibility even though he promised that if it didn't work out between us he would send me back home— since he did make six figures. He said that when we were at the peak of our relationship when we were both happy—sad that it was such an empty promise.

I bought one of my really good friends a ticket to go with me (which I had to charge of course). I couldn't imagine going back out there without any support since that is the way it was everyday while I lived there. I also needed insurance that I wouldn't back down and stay if he tried to woo me back into the black hole of death. I was excited to see the Midwest again but certainly not him. After all we did fight every time we spoke on the phone during my time away.

When my friend and I arrived he acted somewhat like he always did—that everything was ok when it wasn't. How pathetic I thought. I will be as civil as much as my stomach can take. We didn't really spend that much time together over the next couple of days while my friend Angel and I were there. He did, however, hover when we packed acting like I was going to steal one of his precious treasures from high school. If only he hadn't thrown away that hideous lamp with the built in coaster. That would have really shown him and his mother if I took that back with me. This was one item I don't even think a charity would accept knowing that a homeless person would rather have a cardboard box than such a hideous lamp.

I asked him if I could take the bench that we found shortly after I moved in and he started to whine like a child.

"That was something we were supposed to work on together and we never did. I wanted to take it with me so I had something to take my mind off of all of this when I got back." I said.

I thought that he would be nice and tell me I could take it since he was keeping a nice bookshelf we picked out together and some coffee tables. Not the case.

"I really wanted to keep it since I have all of the supplies and since I like to do that kind of work. You don't even know what needs to be done or how to refinish it." He said in a condescending tone.

"Fine, whatever, I am not going to argue about a stupid bench." I said frustrated.

One thing Angel and I found out later well before I made it back was that he stored some of the things we bought together in the basement so I wouldn't find them. Another wonderful form of deceit to uncover later as a parting gift. I thought he was greedy but I hadn't seen him quite like this to be so paranoid that I would actually take something that didn't belong to me.

The day came to pack the huge moving truck for my final departure. A day I think all of us were waiting for in drawn out anticipation. We were in the truck and emotions must have been high because Trevor called and for some disrespectful manner Peter answered the phone, while we were trying to move!

"You still can't give me your complete attention even when I am on the way out?" I said upset.

Of course he got angry again because God forbid you call him out on anything. At that very moment I had a flashback of when we were visiting his parents and his mom was doing something on the computer while he was trying to help her and he snapped at her because she wasn't doing it exactly as he wanted. His mother tried to appease him and ended up saying absolutely nothing like it never happened. This was a mistake she made that I would not make. I guess this is what he expected either from everyone or just women. Unfortunately until my spirit was broken mid way through the relationship I couldn't keep my opinions to myself about his rude behavior. I honestly think he would have preferred women better when they couldn't vote—no female voice is what he preferred. That was not me by any means.

"Why shouldn't I be able to answer my phone?" He snapped.

"Fuck you Peter, you are an asshole." I said.

And boy did that feel good to finally be able to speak my mind without fearing that he would ignore me for days, or that he would sing those awful songs in the morning to taunt me, or use his cheapness to make me feel like a financial burden. I didn't even care who he called anymore or what he said.

So, Angel and I got into my car and made a quick trip to the house and then drove to the local bar about four blocks from the house. As she went to the bathroom, I ordered a rum and coke and then another rum and coke and then a double rum and coke. I hadn't eaten much that day so the liquor absorbed into my blood stream quite nicely. I had confiscated his Jesus on the crucifix in the event that he did anything to my stuff while I was out of the house. I now had his precious Jesus from what I think he me told prior that his dead grandmother gave him. If I was going to hell then it was going to be worth it. I had Jesus, Angel and the rum to keep me company while I progressed towards a comfortable state of numbness.

While I was filling Angel in with all of the insane details that existed in lieu of an actual relationship I got really angry after being quite drunk and dipped Jesus into the nachos we ordered. Jesus was now covered with sour cream and guacamole. One woman down several people from us at the bar couldn't believe I did that to Jesus and made a remark.

"I cannot believe what you are doing." She said.

That opened up the can of worms and it was almost a literal can of worms because something was extremely rotten to the core. I told everyone who would listen in that bar about the jerk that I met, moved to the Midwest for, and who eventually betrayed me after treating me so poorly for so long.

"Shame on him I said, and shame on me for putting up with it."

No one could believe all of his obsessions and how everything had to be a certain way. They couldn't understand how cheap he was when he made decent money. They were so disappointed in the fact that he called himself a good Catholic. They went on to say how ashamed they were in his parents for encouraging him to leave me stranded. They tried to reassure me that those in the Midwest don't treat people like that. They actually felt bad for me. This is what I will miss the most about the Midwest. The people were so friendly and caring.

I even met a couple—at least I thought they were a couple. They seemed very interested in each other.

The way they looked at each other was the way that Peter and I once looked at each other. It seemed like the guy may have had commitment issues because he was somewhat reluctant to talk about their status. So, I felt compelled to give them advice. I told them that life is short and if they care about each other don't rush it by any means but certainly don't waste valuable time that you could be caring for each other. I prayed for them that night in my drunken stooper that they would be happy with or without the other. They seemed like a very nice couple and I wanted to see someone happy even if it isn't me at the moment.

Angel and I eventually went back to the house and I laid down while she took a shower. I was so drunk I think I drooled on Peter's pillow. Peter came home and found me on the bed and asked about dinner. Apparently he thought that we would all do dinner on our last night together even after the fight in the moving truck. When he saw how drunk I was he stormed out and slammed the door. Strangely enough he knew I had his Jesus. How did he memorize where everything was in his house? That attention to detail was from the obsessive compulsive behavior I had come to despise.

After her shower, Angel and I went to a Chinese restaurant around the corner and got dinner. I tried to eat as much as possible because I needed something to absorb the numbing agent I ingested earlier. Peter came home and went upstairs to his bedroom formally known as the office. He pretended everything was ok, something he was really starting to master.

When we were getting ready for bed I was compelled to talk to Peter. I knew this was the last night we would ever see each other. I knew what we were doing was the right thing but it hurt so badly that I hoped speaking to him would make things a little easier.

I started telling him how sorry I was for anything bad that I may have done and I started crying. He said he was sorry too and he grabbed me and held me so tight. I could hear him crying, and for the first time in a long time, I actually believed him when he said he was sorry. We held each other so long we ended up falling asleep together. Finally, a reprieve from the breakup nightmare.

The next day, the day of my final departure I told him that I really could not afford to give him the gifts I gave him for his birthday but I wanted him to keep them. I asked him if he could pay me for them knowing that I have no job and I still have to pay for my monthly bills with what little savings I had left.

He wrote me a check. Wow, I thought, this might be civil after all. I would soon be wrong once again. We ended somehow arguing right before he dropped us off at the airport, I got out grabbed my bag, walked into the airport and never looked back. Hopefully this was the day my new life began.

CHAPTER 13

A new start

Angel and her boyfriend were going to get tattoos the day we got back to my side of the United States and they invited me to go. I didn't feel like doing anything but now that it was truly over I needed to start my life. We went to the tattoo parlor and while we waited I tried to check my messages on my cell phone to find that Peter shut my phone off.

He offered to put me on his plan while we lived together because it was cheaper—go figure. He even reassured me before I left that he would give me reasonable time to get home and get a new phone. How was this reasonable when I just got off of the plane? I couldn't call the phone company mid flight.

I borrowed Angel's phone and called him. That was a big mistake because we fought as if I had never left. He was mad that I left without saying goodbye so he turned off the phone. How immature I thought but I didn't tell him because he would do more damage. Most of my thoughts about him were kept to myself and my friends and family. He agreed to turn the phone back on but only to go back on his word regarding sending my car back for me which would cost an upwards of six hundred dollars. I couldn't believe he was being so cheap even after just receiving a ten to twenty thousand dollar bonus from his work. I think he just wanted to hurt me at this point.

Everyone that could have tried to reason with him did and yet he still refused to pay for the transport of my car even after he gave my mom and me his word. Eventually my parents had to pay for it. My mom was livid yet again. I had no job, almost my entire savings was used to survive when I was looking for a job while living with him because after I moved there he conveniently told me that my preexisting bills were my responsibility not his. I was at a total loss.

At least I had the check he gave me for his birthday presents. I told my parents I could use that to pay for most of the shipping for the car. I would soon be wrong yet again. I went to the bank to cash the check and they advised me that the account had been closed. I stood there in disbelief. I thought things were somewhat civil since we did after all spend our last night together in each other's arms. Doesn't he realize that our actions after that night stemmed from all of the wounds acquired from the battle field over the duration of our so-called relationship?

There was something I had to do now. There was a tattoo I wanted to get for years but he was against them and strongly suggested that he would be very disappointed if I ever got one. Well, now is as good as a time as any. I had a referral to a local artist and I invited a few of my friends to come along for the support. I had already given my picture to the artist and approved what she drew as a stencil now all I needed was the physical part to take place.

The pain from what Peter had done to me was still lingering and I needed something to overpower that feeling. I needed to know that what he did to me was not the most painful thing in the world and I could do whatever I wanted to my body during this new found freedom (within reason of course). It was becoming a great day. I laid down on the bed at the tattoo place and the tattoo artist started the needle. She had to walk me through what she was about to do because I was pretty scared. The tattoo had so much meaning. The tattoo was an African symbol meaning, "Learn from the past." And, that was what I was about to do—learn from my past.

She started to apply the needle to my skin and wowzer the pain was fierce. I couldn't believe how much it actually hurt. It was a nice deviation from the pain lingering from Peter. She was close to a bone during the top part of the design and when she hit it with the needle I felt like I was going to die. Apparently the boney areas are much more sensitive to the needle, as I so painfully discovered. I learned a lot about another kind of pain all too well that evening. Mid way through the process I think my body must have been going into shock because I was completely covered in sweat and my socks were drenched. I had to at one point ask her to stop so I could take off my socks and shoes because I was getting overheated. It was a wonderful process. I was in a different kind of pain now, ready for my new life.

After the brutal attack from the vicious needle and some angry ink we all went to my friend's house to drink margaritas and play games. It was so much fun. I was actually having fun again. I knew I had one last thing to do after my car made it out here safely and that was to disconnect the phone and start over with a new number. I tired to be civil to Peter during the few days my car was still in the Midwest. Surprisingly he agreed to drive it to the location to have it shipped but very sternly reminded us that he would not pay for it to be shipped. Sadly, I think that Peter thought we would actually be friends after all of this. I also think he thought he would still have the phone to hold over my head now that the car is gone. He was the one that would be wrong this time.

The days that passed while my car was being shipped I talked to Peter and pretended things would be civil. I even went so far as to thank him for leaving the phone on. It was amazing how he loved it when I patted him on the back or gave him compliments. He just ate it up, it seemed too easy.

All the while I was grinning and bearing it like our last few intimate moments when all I was thinking about was Trevor, his lovely brown eyed friend. Even as mad as I got with Peter I never confessed my attraction to Trevor. When I was cleaning houses on the side while living with Peter he managed to get Trevor to agree to using my services. Later I found out that he was trying to discourage me from starting my own cleaning business by sending me to Trevor's dirty apartment. I didn't mind cleaning Trevor's house and getting to make his bed and fantasize what my life could have been like had I met him instead. Peter actually thought it was a chore for me.

For some reason I don't think Trevor liked me very much. It may have stemmed from Peter complaining about me and Trevor never hearing my side. But, that didn't bother me because he was so good looking I took anytime with him as awkward as it was to appreciate his beautiful brown eyes. It was sad that I even had these thoughts. To my defense I was lonely, my boyfriend hardly paid attention to me, and the only time I could see him lately was to spend time with him and his friends.

Sometimes I wondered what it would have been like if I met Trevor first. Would things be more normal? Was Trevor easier going? Trevor seemed more normal to me at this point. Heck, the crazy guy that hangs out off of the freeway with a cardboard sign seems more normal to me than Peter. He would probably be grateful for a clean box/house and dinner.

My car finally arrived and I was excited now more than hurting. My tattoo was healing and so was my heart, both a lot slower than I wished. I knew this was the second to last step to my freedom. I needed closure so badly now that I was starting over. After getting in my car I drove myself to the cell phone store and walked in so proud and determined. I don't think the sales guy at the store realized that he was providing me with a much needed freedom similar to that of a newly released inmate of prison after several years of solitary confinement. I could hear the clock ticking on the wall in the store while I waited for him to process my request. He couldn't type fast enough because my victory would be getting the new phone activated before Peter could exhibit what little control he had left over me. It was going to be a great day. All I kept saying to myself in my head was, Hurry up man, hurry up." It was truly a nail biting experience. I probably would have bitten all of my nails off if I didn't have my tattoo throbbing under my clothes still trying to heal.

It has been done. I am now a completely free woman. I have my phone, my new phone number and I walked out of the cell phone store with so much enthusiasm I almost for a moment wondered what I would do with all of that adrenaline. And then it hit me, I would call all of my friends and family and celebrate with my new phone service.

I couldn't shut off the previous phone service because it was under Peter's name. So, I left it on and said nothing to him. I figured he would soon enough realize that the phone was not being used and he could shut it off at that time. I guess he didn't realize for a while and ended up sending me an email.

> *"I am not sure how to begin. I want to know how you are doing. I want to tell you how I have been but I am not sure you want to hear from me. You were right when you said this would be the hardest thing to do. I feel like my best friend has died.*
>
> *I know things ended badly between us but I wish there was some way that we could become friends again because you are a really good person. I wish you could still be in my life.*
>
> *Peter*
>
> *PS: Can you tell me when you get a new phone*

This email came almost as surprising as the very first email he sent me. Was I nostalgic? No. Was I sad? No, not anymore. The anger did rush to my fingertips and I ended up writing this email to him:

"You are a fool if you think we will ever be friends. Friends do not treat each other the way you treated me. The way you sold me out to your friends and family when you were having a hard time with the relationship, the way you poked and prodded at me like I was a toy, the way you resisted my affection in a joking manner because you thought it was funny.

You are a virus Peter, you and your fucked up family . . . I believe it was the right thing to do too . . . . the very fact that you would accept your b-day presents from me shows me how DESPICABLE of a person you are . . . you think you were entitled to those presents? You weren't . . . I wish I never gave them to you and I hope to hell that every time you open that wallet to count your precious money you remember who gave it to you and what it really cost—OUR FRIENDSHIP!!!

Then, you write me a check that you recind on . . . . WTF!!!!! You gave me your word.

You lied to me about New York, you were going to leave me stranded and practically destitute in the Midwest, you accepted gifts from me knowing that I would need that money later, you went back on your word about the car, you wrote me a bad check . . . . WHY IN THE HELL WOULD I EVER WANT TO BE FRIENDS WITH SOMEONE LIKE YOU???????

I am so sorry I met you and I am disgusted by the very fact that you are still a memory for me (which hopefully soon will change).

I wish things could have been different . . . I wished you could have been a better person . . . I begged you to be a better person when we were separating . . . but you decided not to be . . . shame on you . . . shame on you . . . .

Everyone I meet and everyone I spend my time with will get to see the good side of me and enjoy my friendship . . . my unending, giving friendship— you will not!! You had such a good person by your side . . . someone that would have done anything for you . . . . Anything Peter.

Goodbye forever!!!

Surprisingly enough I did not send that email after all of that wonderful venting and effort. I realized if I let Peter get me that angry again he will see that I still have some type of feelings for him even if it is pain. That is not what I wanted. As soon as I took back control of my life and worked towards a happy destiny I could start living and Peter would become more of a distant memory.

The curser blinked for what seemed like a hundred times waiting for me to write something after I deleted this horrible email. It sure did feel good to get it all out though. But, I was damned if I was going to be like the horrible person I saw in Peter. The virus needed to be stopped, even if it didn't stop with him it would stop with me. That is not who I was before I met Peter and I certainly was not going to let him rob me of my wonderful identity pre-Peter.

I took a deep breath and started typing. My final response said:

"Please do not contact me anymore."

It was just as simple as that. Very specific and very final. I never truly appreciated the word final until that day. A smile appeared on my face as I blocked all of his email addresses from my account just in case he tried to contact me after that. My new found freedom and identity were awaiting my attention. Enough time had been spent on Peter. My new life was waiting and the wait was finally over.

CHAPTER 14

Baby steps

Several weeks had gone by and I was getting used to being by myself again. It was nice to be able to do whatever I wanted when I wanted and not feel guilty about it. I was working two jobs, a full time job and my part time retail job. I was making really good money now and was able to pay off most of my bills and start saving for my future.

I still couldn't get the Mid-West out of my mind. I thought that if I started saving I could eventually make my way back there. I wouldn't go back to the same place where Peter and I were but I could at least end up in the Mid-West somewhere.

I was working seven days a week trying to save and put the awful memories behind me. After a couple of months I could feel the fatigue from working two jobs and I started getting sick. Maybe my immune system was still week from all of the stress and mourning. Maybe it wasn't the best idea to work two jobs so quickly. I started feeling like I had the flu so I decided to take a couple of days off from both jobs. I started to feel a little bit better but then about a week later I was sick again. I started to convince myself that maybe two jobs was just too much for me at this time. I actually considered quitting my part time job that I loved so much.

Then, that is when it hit me. I noticed that I was only getting sick in the mornings and most of the time it would pass and I would feel better. It was almost a constant process of feeling sick in the morning and then later feeling better and more like myself. I told a couple of my friends and they jokingly said that I was pregnant. I told them that it couldn't be. I would know if I was pregnant and I was on the pill the entire time I was with Peter. So, why then am I not feeling well so often? I then remembered something I tried to suppress since last talking to Peter, we were intimate our last night together before I left his house to come home. What was I thinking back then? How could my luck be so bad? I guess he didn't listen to his father's advice on the phone after all.

After a few more days of feeling horrible I went to the grocery store and purchased a pregnancy test. I couldn't believe that I was actually considering this. However, I wanted to rule it out before panicking and going o the doctor.

The test said to wait until the morning because there is a higher accuracy rate so I waited. I laid in my bed that night wondering what I would do if I was pregnant. Could I take raising a child who reminded me of someone so awful? What was I going to do?

The next morning I woke up in shear panic and went into the bathroom to do the deed? I sat down and took the test. I then waited the longest few minutes in my life. I sat there tired and in disbelief. I wanted to look before the time was up but didn't want to jinx myself.

Time was up. It was time to look. I grabbed the test and sure enough it was positive. This is why I have been so tired, sick and emotional. Will I keep this baby? I know one thing for sure and that is that Peter will never find out.

Printed in the United States
By Bookmasters